T0354761

The Storyteller

Other books by Tom Edwards:

If I should die *
No greater freedom*
Lethal legacy *
The Fifinella log
The story teller
Jane Sinclair*
The Honourable Catherine*
Undercurrent – Vengeance is mine.
Tom – the adventures of a Portsmouth lad
Technical:
DIY Guide to international accreditation for companies Pt 1 & pt 2
Undercover

• Reader's Choice Award, or other awards.

The Storyteller

Tom Edwards

THE STORYTELLER

iUniverse books may be ordered through booksellers or by contacting:

iUniverse
1663 Liberty Drive
Bloomington, IN 47403
www.iuniverse.com
1-800-Authors (1-800-288-4677)

ISBN: 978-1-5320-6539-2 (sc)
ISBN: 978-1-5320-6540-8 (e)

Print information available on the last page.

iUniverse rev. date: 12/28/2018

This book is dedicated to my brother Ken for his humour and stoicism under extreme duress – always my inspiration.
Tom

Contents

Introduction

This is a series of short stories, most of which have a sting in the tail. The only true story is 'The Entomologist' and the rest have been embellished and are purely fictional

The first story, The 'Entomologist' and the conversation, full of malapropisms, actually occurred. Frappin' the Wurzel on the other hand is entirely a figment of the authors imagination and depicts George, a bucolic arcadian in a small English pub who, in an effort to maintain his reputation as the village prankster, exploits the very obvious charms of an American tourist – an activity that would probably get him thrown in goal in a more enlightened society. 'Spider Loves Me' and 'A Near Gaff' introduces pathos into the mix and most of the other stories have an unexpected ending that may intrigue or amuse the reader.

The title of this book was inadvertently suggested to me by a charming lady whilst I was giving a talk to a library group. I had been narrating various yarns of events that had occurred during my lifetime and my audience appeared to enjoy them. During the tea break the lady had approached me remarking, "You *are* a storyteller!" I placed the wrong connotation on her comment and protested that they were all true, most of which have been modified to comply with libel laws, She hurriedly corrected my misunderstanding saying that she enjoyed my tales and that I should set them down in a book; this I have done.

Many of the stories have an element of truth, painfully so. However some are figments of my imagination and some have been enhanced to give them humour or pathos; most have a twist in the tail that may surprise or amuse the reader. I do hope you enjoy them.

Tom Edwards

The 'Entomologist'

It was a dark and dismal day and New Zealand lived up to its reputation as *the land of the long white cloud* – except that there were no clouds visible at all through the driving rain that lashed, almost horizontally at the building site, driven by a ferocious wind that snaked and curled around the temporary structures causing them to rock and rattle on their equally temporary foundations.

A bus sat heavily in the muddy yard, its windows fogged and the slow metronomic swishing of its wipers indicating that there was possibly life within, not that any sign was discernible from the outside.

At irregular intervals men would dash from various offices and workshops around the yard pulling on heavy-weather coats or totally inadequate spray jackets; their pounding boots sending a spray of mud and water from the quickly growing pools that threatened to link up and cover the entire area. They leaped onto the steps of the bus that rocked and groaned with ancient decrepitude, and disappeared into the fetid interior.

Tom stood in the doorway of the site-office hoping for a break in the rain that would enable him to reach the bus without being soaked to the skin. The Minivan that he usually drove into Auckland was in the site workshop for an overdue service and he had left his heavy weather gear on the back seat.

He reflected on the circumstances that had brought him to that inclement land. Sailing around the world in a thirty foot boat that was badly damaged in a storm off the Bay of Plenty, and the subsequent necessity to earn enough money to repair his boat and resume his journey. His job as an engineer on the Huntley Power Station paid well and another few weeks would see his boat repaired and refitted so that he could continue his trip. Only a few months previously he had been acclimatising to the heat and high humidity of Australia's northern coast, now he shivered in the wet cold winter of New Zealand. He took a deep breath, bent his head down and made a frantic dash for the bus which seemed ready to depart.

Entering the bus took more that just the physical effort. The stench of wet clothing and sweaty bodies hung suspended in the cigarette smoke that filled the interior; trapped inside the closed windows. Short bursts of phlegmy coughing sent the smoke swirling in swirling eddies around the afflicted. Tom peered into the gloom searching for an empty seat. He moved forward to where a thin gnome-like man sat and Tom looked at him askance. The man finally glanced up and with some reluctance removed his backpack from the seat and dropped it on the floor between his legs. Tom smiled his thanks and sat down; the man made no comment and turned to gaze out of the window.

"Not very nice weather!" Tom remarked pleasantly. The man glanced briefly at Tom and muttered some indistinct comment, which to Tom's ears sounded vaguely Germanic.

'Another one of the many foreign labourers working on the project,' Tom mused to himself. They comprised the major part of the workforce of several hundred men.

The bus gave a couple of spasmodic heaves and the smell of used diesel fumes wafted in through the rear door before it began to close, sealing out any possibility of fresh air. It seemed to Tom an improvement on the miasma that was already there.

Tom surreptitiously studied his companion as he stared out of the window. From time to time he used the sleeve of his jacket to clear a small opening on the fogged-up glass through which to peer at the passing scene. He had a thin face and a long narrow nose. His face was swarthy, with several days' growth of beard darkening his cheeks and chin. He had a black shapeless hat pulled low around his ears that looked as if it had been a trilby in its better days, but now resembled an old mob-cap; it had a greenish tinge in the dim light. He wore a bright yellow site-issue spray-coat two sizes too small, even for his meagre frame, allowing the frayed cuffs of his jacket to protrude at the wrists. Tom judged him to be in his early fifties.

"Terrible weather we're having," he tried again, "only a few months ago I was up in Darwin, North Australia; a bit different from this, it was nearly forty degrees up there!"

The man dragged his nose away from the porthole. "Ah! Yes, Oi know, it gets roit hot up dar. But it's not so mooch da heat, it's da *'humility'* dat gets yer." He turned back to the window.

Tom recognised the very broad Irish accent and realised his earlier mistake regarding the man's origins. He watched him for a while wondering if he knew he had just uttered a malapropism, but there appeared to be no humour in the man sitting alongside of him.

"Yes! I agree with you there, the ..." he paused. He was going to say 'humidity' but did not wish to embarrass the man. "The..ahh... moisture in the air makes a difference doesn't it?" He finished lamely.

The man spoke without turning. "Dat's roit. Oi've got a smaall place in town 'n' when Oi'm loyin in me bed at noit Oi can see da *'condescension'* runnin' down da winders, so Oi can."

Tom looked at him sharply to try to ascertain if the Irishman was doing it deliberately, but his face held only the same blank look as before. There was not the slightest hint of a smile. Was he trying to get a rise out of him? He couldn't tell.

"Of course, dat Darwin, it's a long way furder nort!" He continued after a pause. "An' da *attitude* makes a difference, ye see! It's nearer to da *ecuador.*"

Tom shifted in his seat; uncertainty making him irritated.

"Yes!" he replied with some asperity. "It's only about twelve degrees south *latitude* there. We're almost thirty-seven here. Darwin is much closer to the *equator!*" He replied callously, emphasising the two words.

The Irishman appeared not to notice.

Having vented his spleen Tom regretted his cruel attack. After all not too many people were etymologists, or even had the same chance as he, of a good education. He felt embarrassed by his lack of feeling and understanding He thought to apologise but as the man seemed not to have noticed he let the moment pass.

"Have you been working on the site long?" Tom asked, by way of healing any perceived affront.

"Ah sure! me an' me pals arrived here roit aat da beginnin' loik. Dey was jist startin' to set out da site den. Yes," he mused. "We were roit here at its *deception* we were, and Oi tink we'll be here at da finish."

Tom studied the man's profile, attempting to find any signs of duplicity, but saw only tired resignation. The look of a man who had seen the worst life had to offer and expected no relief.

Tom changed the subject. "I see you've got a woman for Prime Minister now! What do you think of that? Did you vote for her?" He smiled.

There was silence for a while, then the Irishman turned to Tom with a shrug. "Ah! It don't bodder me none, she can't do any worse dan da last lot!" He paused for a while. "Oi have nuttin to do wid dat lot, whoever's in don't make no difference to da loiks of me. Yas can *abject* as mooch as yas loik but it makes no difference, so why bodder?" He seemed to warm to the conversation. "You've done a bit of travelin' den, 'ave ya? Ya moost 'ave seen a fair bit o' da world den!"

Tom, like most adventurers, enjoyed recounting stories of his travels and for the next ten minutes he hardly drew a breath. Realizing that he was hogging the conversation he smiled ruefully.

"I'm sorry, I get carried away sometimes!" he said. "I'm probably boring you to death, you should have stopped me."

"Not aat aall lad, Oi loik ta hear odder people's *antidotes;* very interesting," he said kindly. "I wish Oidda done summit loik it meself." He turned back to the window.

By this time the bus was crawling painfully up the hill to Tom's stop. He eased himself out of his seat. "Well, cheerio! It's been... interesting talking to you" he said with a smile. Then some puckish whim took over and he added "The way those politicians carry on is terrible, you're quite right. No wonder we all become *septics.*"

He grinned at the Irishman. As he turned to leave the Irishman detained him with a gentle hand on his arm.

"Oi don't want to offend yas lad" he said, with a deferential look, "but da word yas was wanting was sceptics. Septic means that somtin' is rotten loik. Yees used da wrong word. No offence intended, Oi taught yas would want to know." He turned back to the window and as Tom went to move off he heard him mutter, "Geesus! Don't dey teach dem nuttin' in school dees days?"

Tom stood on the pavement shaking his head. He looked back at the bus but the Irishman was gazing out of the window and didn't acknowledge his salute.

The Skellum*

Bill drove slowly down the circular driveway that led to the house; he rubbed his hand wearily across his stubbled jaw and pushed his bush cap to the back of his head. Pulling up in front of the path that led to the house he reached behind him for the backpack and rifle that resided on the back seat. Swinging the pack strap over his shoulder he walked slowly down the path to the rear door that opened onto the kitchen. He had hardly stepped through the door when Sabina, the cook and house girl, relieved him of his burdens and stacked them in a corner where she knew that, when he was ready, he would clean them himself.

She looked at him noting the tired lines around his eyes and she tutted in a soft croon, "Ah, boss, you stink bad. I got yo favrit stew when yo ready. He smiled gratefully as his nose picked up the scent of kudu wafting from the pot. He sat down heavily on a rough wooden bench as Sabina eased her considerable bulk down onto the floor and began unlacing his veltskoens. The boots were badly scuffed and caked with mud from the many miles of tracking over the past two weeks. She removed the boots with a mighty heave and recoiled at the smell that pervaded the kitchen.

"Ah, boss", she wailed, "I think yo feets is too sick". She laughed, having performed this same function many times before.

The small farm was situated in the north east corner of the country, near Mtoko and only a few miles from the Mozambique border, from where most of the terrorists infiltrated the country. Many farms had been attacked and many white farmers had long since departed the country, but Bill hung on with fierce determination, even though he realised that the battle was long lost.

Sabina reached up under his trousers and pulled down his socks that felt damp and sticky and with a shudder of distaste dropped them on the floor where they stuck emitting an obscene odour.

"Yo bath is ready, boss". She said.

Bill knew it would be. She appeared to have some arcane knowledge as to when he would appear back from patrol and a hot steaming bath would be ready with an abundance of bath salts to cut through the grime that covered his body. He rose slowly and padded down the hallway to the bathroom, shedding his clothes as he went. His feet made sticky marks on the polished floor behind him. He eased his aching body into the tub with a short grunt of pleasure as he sunk slowly under the layer of bubbles. He surfaced with an explosive snort and lay quietly thinking of the past weeks.

It had begun two days before the actual patrol started, with mock battles, shooting at targets hidden in the dense bush. There had been first-aid lectures where they had been shown how to plug a bullet hole in the chest with a tampon dipped in the casualty's blood to make it easier to insert. They had practiced inserting a cannula into a vein to introduce a drip and how to tie a pressure bandage on an amputated limb. They had lined up their weapons on a target range and ran, ran, ran. They had not been allowed to wash with soap, then, or for the following two weeks, as the smell could be detected in the heavy air of the jungle giving an enemy warning of their presence.

He smiled as he recalled the day he left. He had stowed his pack on the back seat of his car, ensuring that the two water bottles were full; the six full magazines were taped in reversed pairs to facilitate a quick change-over, and that there was five hundred additional rounds for his FN rifle. He had cautioned Sabina to take care of the house, promising her a bonsala, a gift, if everything was in good order when he returned. As he started the car he called Kingston, the head gardener to him repeating the same promise of a bonsala if all was well when he returned. As he began to move off Kingston had dashed up calling out, "Baas, can I have my bonsala now?" Bill told him, no! He would have to wait until he returned. Kingston blurted, "But, boss, what if you don't come back?"

As he drove off Bill had called back, "You take your chances the same as me! You skellum!"

He recalled the many times he had threatened to fire Kingston over the past sixteen years. There had been times when he would have done so and many more times when he had chased him with a pickaxe handle with every intention of breaking a few bones. He often disappeared for days on end to return to his tribe to bury his 'father'; of which there seemed to be an endless number. All the men who were initiated together as youths were considered brothers, and as such were honorary 'fathers' to each other's children. He had pleaded with Bill to give him gumboots and an extra blanket during the cold, rainy season. Bill had done so, only to discover five days later that he had sold them for *u-ɗhwala*, the native beer. He smiled as he recalled the way Kingston had reacted when he almost trod on a boomslang that was basking on the hot ground. He had given a wild shriek and leaped about six feet in the air. Bill had planted his boot on the creature's neck and quickly severed its head with his panga. For a week after he had tormented the gardener with taunts, calling him *iɗi khukhukazi*, a chicken, and *i-gwala*, a coward. He had stopped when he realised that Kingston was deeply ashamed of his reaction. His tribal family were Shangaans, who had a very brave tradition as warriors. For weeks after he had taken quite unnecessary risks with snakes and other wild creatures in an attempt to convince Bill of his bravery.

He had fallen asleep when Sabina returned fifteen minutes later. Without any comment she raised one foot and proceeded to scrub it gently, endeavouring to remove the ingrained dirt from his heels and toes. Then she took out a small knife and cleaned out his toenails; he would have to trim them later. She did the same with the other foot and scrubbed up as far as his knees before attending to his hair which she covered with shampoo and worked it thoroughly into the scalp. Then using a ladle she rinsed it off and began on his back which was badly scarred from thorn bushes and rocks. She flannelled the septic cuts until they bled and patted them dry with a clean cloth. Finally he stepped out of the bath and waited as Sabina let the filthy water out and cleaned the tub prior to refilling it and adding yet more bath salts. Bill stepped back into the water and revelled in the comfort and cleanness. Ten minutes later Sabina returned with a pot of ointment and when Bill had dried himself she applied the unction to the cuts and scratches on his back, then handed him the pot for him to treat the various rashes that spawned from armpits and groin.

He slipped into his pajamas and dressing gown and hurried with anticipation to the dining room and the kudu stew. Sabina knew well that when he returned from patrol his appetite was much diminished for the first few days, but she always made a huge quantity of stew anyway. What he did not eat she and Kingston, and the other workers would finish off.

Completing his meal he wandered out onto the stoep and stood admiring the grand view down the valley to the Shamva Mountains, purple in the distance. He poured himself a 'special' from the icy jug that he knew would be there, and sipped it gratefully as he sank into a wicker chair. Sabina's 'specials' were renown, or had been, in the area; always ready when visitors arrived. Her own concoction, it consisted of a tall cold glass with four cubes of ice in the bottom. These were covered with lemon juice followed by one jigger of Gordon's Gin and one and a half jiggers of Cinzano Bianco, topped up with tonic water and swizzled. It was delicious, especially on a hot day. Having finished several drinks he retired to his bed where he slept until noon the following day.

Two days later, having fully recovered Bill drove into town to replace supplies that had been greatly diminished over the past weeks. He bought enough meat and maize flour for the workforce, sugar, tea and all those things that a quick stocktake had shown were sadly depleted. He restocked the stoep fridge with his favourite beer and carried out a tour of inspection of the farm to see how it had been managed without him. The farm had long ago been cleared of animals, apart from a few that were kept close to the homestead, and was now reduced to growing food mainly for local consumption. Several days passed before he became aware that his supplies were diminishing faster than they should be. For some time he had made a habit of remembering the pattern of sugar cubes in the box. He had taken four cubes from the centre of a layer. The next time he made tea the pattern was the same but inexplicably the box was empty within a few days. Then he realised that entire layers had been removed and the same pattern maintained. He was quite attuned to the normal minor pilfering but this was excessive. He trusted Sabina implicitly but had caught Kingston coming out of the kitchen once before when she was hanging clothes in the yard but could prove nothing. He turned his bottle of whisky upside down and checked the level of spirit. He knew that Kingston would look for a mark if the bottle was up the right way. When Sabina had retired to her kia for the night Bill removed all the ration packs from the fridge and numbered them from 1 to 30 in small numbers on the bottom and replaced them, then he counted the tea bags in the opened packet. Three days later it was obvious that he was losing tea, sugar and meat; packages 17 and 11 were missing from the stoep fridge and the tea bags much depleted.

He called to Kingston who was cleaning the swimming pool.

"Kingston, you skellum, come here!"

He grabbed him by the ear and pulled his face close. "You've been stealing my meat, sugar and tea, and probably much more and you're going to pay for them."

Kingston adopted a pained, hard done by look; his eyes wide and innocent.

"Icona, baas, iseko indaba.' No boss, no problem. He protested his innocence, waving his arms with every sign of outraged incorruptibility. Bill had seen it all before on many occasions and was not convinced.

"You're lying again." He roared. Twisting his ear.

"Icona, baas!" He repeated as he twisted his head free of Bill's grip. As he turned away Bill caught a fleeting grin appear momentarily on his face.

"Bloody kaffirs!" He muttered as he watched Kingston's jaunty swagger as he walked back to the pool.

The farm labourers, like most Africans usually ate twice a day; at 10am and 6pm; the latter being their main meal. Kingston, whose job kept him near the house, usually had his meals cooked by Sabina, who handed it to him on his tin plate. That evening Bill intercepted her and informed her that he would be giving Kingston his meal. She made no comment.

In that part of Africa, for many reasons there were often endemic bladder infections among the whites. The usual treatment was to take Dr MacKenzies Veinoids, which was a similar pill as is sold in England as Carters Little Liver Pills. The effect of these pills is to turn the urine bright green. Bill inserted three of these pills into Kingston's meal and covered them up with the thick gravy. As he handed the meal to the gardener he again challenged him and again received a vigorous denial.

"If you are lying, you skellum," he said briefly, "your wee will turn bright green and you will die!"

"Ja, boss, he muttered offhandedly, as he seated himself on the garden wall to eat his meal.

Later that day, whilst Bill was working in the lower field, Kingston came running down the hill.

"Baas. Bass! I have been stealing yo meat and yo sugar and yo tea and yo beer..."

"I didn't know about that one," muttered Bill.

"My wee is so greenie, Bass, Am I goin' to die?"

"I bloody well hope so, you skellum!" Bill muttered.

It was two days prior to Bill reporting to his unit in preparation for another patrol. He was in the habit of sleeping lightly where the slightest noise wakened him; a reflex action of self preservation. A soft scratching on the bedroom window saw him roll quietly off the bed and reach for his FN. He signalled Kingston to go to the back door as he slipped into his veltskoons and joined him, dragging him into the darkened kitchen. "Maningi indaba, Bass," he hissed. Big trouble! He pointed towards the fence behind the kias, the native huts. "Terrorists are cutting through the fence; there are about ten of them.

Bill wasted no time, and patting him on the shoulder by way of thanks, he reached for the Agric Alert and pressed the button. This was an emergency alarm that would inform all his neighbours that his farm was under attack. Within minutes they would be on full alert and all available help would be on its way. He slipped out of the door behind Kingston as he heard the first piercing scream from one of the native girls in the worker's village.

He knew the path well and moved quickly and silently. He heard Sabina beginning a high pitched keening and broke into a run regardless of the noise of his approach. Sabina, as with most of his workers had been in his employ for many years; some had worked for his father. He considered Sabina more of a friend than a servant and his anger spurred him on. He broke into the clearing where there were a cluster of kias and took the scene in with a quick glance. Maria, Sabina's assistant in the house was in the process of being raped by three of the terrorists; she was fighting for her life as she knew that when they had finished with her she would have her stomach opened up with a panga as was their practice. Sabina had gone to her assistance and was fighting off two thugs who were screaming with laughter as they pushed her from one to the other. The rest of the workers had been herded into a cowering group near a burning kia.

Bill opened fire, double tapping in quick succession; the terrorists fell under the withering fire. The survivors began to run back towards the broken fence; those attacking the girl jumped to their feet and followed. That was when Bill's ammunition ran out, as did his luck. He stood there for a while dumfounded and cursed as he realised that he had not refilled the magazine since he had returned from patrol – an action he normally carried out automatically. The twenty shot magazine had been half empty. He swore an oath as he grabbed the gun by the barrel to use as a club. The terrorists soon realised that the situation had changed and with whoops of joy returned to the attack. Five lay dead or dying on the ground but that still left seven, two of which appeared to be wounded. They closed in for the kill.

As the first of the attackers reached him Bill swung the rifle in a scything arc that connected with the leader's skull with a sickening crunch that removed half his head; he spun to the ground. The others closed in, two of them angling to get behind him. He rushed at another and smashed the butt of his weapon into his face and saw the man reel back with blood pouring from his wound, then they were on him. He managed to wrestle a panga from the hand of one but before he could use it he felt a terrible blow across his back and felt his left arm going numb. The only thing that saved him in the next few minutes was their closeness; they were too close to use their weapons effectively.

He felt his senses reeling and realised that the end was near. It was then that he saw Kingston dash from the cover of the trees and snatch up a panga from a dead terrorist. With a wild war cry from the inbred memory of his Shangaan ancestors he entered the fray. He cleaved the head of the man behind Bill who was about to land another blow and swung around to cover Bill's back. Bill felt a surge of renewed hope as he hacked and sliced; his left arm hanging uselessly at his side. They were still hopelessly outnumbered but they fought on. No whoops now just stentorian gasps and grunts. He heard Kingston cry out but had no time to look as he fended off blow after blow. Then from out of the trees came a withering fire as three of his neighbours from the adjacent farm joined the battle. It was soon over. Bill sagged to the ground totally exhausted. He heard the wounded being finished off by his rescuers – the time for mercy had long passed. He passed out from loss of blood for a short period and he regained his senses as Sabina removed his pyjama jacket to tend his wounds. He pushed her aside and staggered to his feet as he saw the body of Kingston lying on the blood-soaked grass where he had fallen. He kneeled beside him and cradled his head in the crook of his one good arm as the others gathered around.

Kingston was barely alive as blood poured from a badly damaged artery in his neck. Bill balled up his jacket and attempted to stem the flow, knowing as he did so that it was hopeless. He held him as his life ebbed and for a while was unable to speak as his throat constricted with unshed tears.

"Why did you have to do that for, you skellum?" He croaked. "You could have got away."

"Ah, Baas." He whispered as Bill leaned forward to catch his words. "Did I fight well?"

"Like ten *m'khulu* Shangaan warriors." Bill replied in a choked voice. Then he felt Kingston relax in his arms.

* South African word for a rogue

The Baobab Tree

Bluey Wilkins had originated from Newcastle, New South Wales. He was not a very pleasant character, but he did have a cheerfully rough way about him that helped him to fit into the sort of environment in which he now found himself. In Australia those who didn't know him too well would have called him a 'bit of a larrikin'.

He was a tall skinny bloke with a mop of carroty coloured hair that stuck up like a bristle brush. Bluey wasn't his real name of course. His red hair had laid that sobriquet on him in that strange arcane way that Aussies have. In his mid fifties, he was still fairly healthy although his propensity for booze, women and 'rollies' had taken their toll.

Bluey had worked for a number of years at the coal-face of a dozen different mines along the Hunter Valley. He had a quite surprising effect on women. None of his mates could understand what they saw in him, but you could never catch sight of Bluey in the local pub without a woman fussing about him. That was his big problem, really. He decided to try his luck on the mines in the wilds of Angola, just ahead of three paternity suits.

The mine itself was really an exploratory drilling site to see if there was sufficient copper ore to make the project viable. Copper mines, of course had been operating along the 'Copper Belt' in Zambia for many years but it would appear that the ore there had a use-by date. There was a closer mine still operating as a viable entity to the north of the Namib Desert in, strangely enough, Namibia. The Tsumeb mine in Namibia was the nearest one to Angola, so it was from there that that the advance party was sent to set up the proving site. Bluey arrived about a month behind the advance party.

The camp itself was set up with the approval of the Angolan government; unfortunately the spot chosen for the site was well outside the area where the government had any possible hope of control. For some thirty years a guerrilla war had waged spasmodically over the whole east and south-east corner of the country and it was virtually a no-go area. The advance party was aware of this fact and were, understandably, somewhat nervous. In fairly close proximity to the site there were native tribes still living in their primitive state; they were also nervous, having been shot at by those on both sides of the conflict for most of their lives.

Into this fragile hot-pot, one steaming hot day, arrived Bluey. The arrival of anyone to that remote, rat-infested, malaria-ridden outpost was a matter of some consequence. The imminent arrival of the supply helicopter, together with an additional worker, had been radioed ahead; it not only heralded a re-supply of booze but it became a *cause célèbre*. So it was that the whole workforce turned out to greet the newcomer and to unload the supplies.

The sight that met Bluey when he stepped down from the chopper was not a prepossessing one. The landing pad that had been hacked out of the jungle was minimal and left very little room for pilot error. Some fifty yards away stood a large pole and mud hut, obviously native built, with a water tank to one side. Other rough outbuildings had been added to house the supplies, the technical equipment and sleeping quarters. Bluey grinned. He had existed in worse digs than that in the Australian outback – he was unfazed. What turned his grin into a derisive laugh however was the sight of the group heading towards him.

They were a rough lot, even bearing in mind that the place they had chosen to work did not lend itself to sartorial elegance. The group consisted of surveyors, a geophysicist, mining engineers, a cook and others. All were inured to living for short periods in the remotest corners of the earth in the frenetic rush for minerals and oil. They all wore long jungle-green trousers tucked into boots, and a whole miscellany of long sleeved shirts, some dirty and all badly sweat stained. However, what they all had in common, and what gave rise to Bluey's derisive mirth, was their hats. Bluey was well acquainted with hats. He had worn the same battered Akubra for over forty years; some reckoned he wore it in bed. It had long ago lost the decorative plaited leather band – anyhow he had no time for that sort of adornment. The men approaching wore hats that were quite common in Africa and attracted no special attention. They were wide brimmed, not unlike the Australian hat, but what made them the object of Bluey's attention was the wide band of leopard skin used as a hat band. In Bluey's mind they conjured up echoes of privilege and wealth, of safaris and shooting lions and tigers with powerful rifles with telescopic sights from the safety of hides. Apart from that they were effeminate!

"Well, well, then! Look at all the big white hunters!" He taunted them by way of introduction; a greeting that endeared him to none. They walked up pleasantly to shake his hand and welcome him. But Bluey had never learned when to stop his banter. They soon tired of him and began unloading the supplies.

Bluey's job was that of general helper and guard. He was to assist the surveyor in mapping the area and provide assistance wherever it was required. He also carried a rifle to guard the camp. In both of these functions he proved uncooperative and aggressive.

One day whilst in the store he espied a bundle of bright yellow marker flags. Working quickly he cut one into three-inch widths about three feet long. Borrowing a stapler from the office he stapled the cloth around his hat, allowing the long tails to hang down his back. When he appeared the others looked at his grinning face but made no comment. They all knew that this was yet another deliberate irritation. De Wit made a mental note to have him sent back to wherever he came from as soon as the next supply chopper arrived.

Most evenings, having finished their meal, they would sit around the multi-purpose table playing cards and discussing the day's work program for the morrow. They were all heavy drinkers but seemed to be able to handle it better than did Bluey, who became more annoying as the night wore on. A week passed and everyone was drinking more than usual – mostly to blot out Bluey's constant banter.

As soon as darkness descended the sound of drums took over from the cicadas. It was an insidious beat, not overloud but always there as a backdrop to all conversation. It seemed to pick up their heartbeat and slowly increase it until they found themselves panting and had to make a deliberate effort to exclude it. The drums came from villages on both sides, about a mile away. None of them had ventured that far, not since an event that had occurred a few weeks prior to their arrival.

A report had arrived from some itinerant prospector informing the corporation that he had found native copper, and the flowers that were usually found in copper bearing areas namely Haumaniastrum katangense and Becium homblei. These cuprophytes are found exclusively on soils bearing copper. Commonly called copper flowers The location was in that corner of Angola. It had excited little interest amongst the board members, until somebody mentioned the magic words, 'dwindling supplies'. The Angolan government was contacted and permission obtained for them to send three experts to the area to give an assessment. During the course of their wanderings they had discovered a huge baobab tree, all the lower branches of which were decorated with skulls, bones and a whole miscellany of mysterious objects. Assuming it to have religious connotations for the local tribes, they had given it a wide berth.

Several days had passed and each night they had heard the steady beat of the drums. De Wit, the South African engineer, and Gert Hofer, the surveyor, accepted it as a normal part of Africa, but Sanderson, an Englishman, became infuriated. All of them drank a great deal but Sanderson began to pour the whisky down his throat in an effort to drown out the insidious beat. It became an obsession, a *bete noire* that tormented him to distraction. Then one afternoon, still half drunk, he screamed obscenities at the surrounding bush and dashing into the explosives store he grabbed four sticks of blasting dynamite, fuses and detonators and headed off towards the baobab tree. De Wit had hurried off to find Hofer but by the time he bumped into him returning down a track the daylight was fading fast, and neither relished chasing after Sanderson in the dark. The drums started up early that night and to their ears they sounded louder and wilder. In the morning they went looking for their companion. As they approached the tree they could see what looked like a ragged bundle on the ground. It was Sanderson. He was terribly mutilated and on his face was etched an expression of absolute terror.

The story got around and lost nothing in the telling. Gert and De Wit had returned but nothing would induce the current team to venture out at night.

It was Gert who inadvertently started the events which followed. They were all deep in their cups, a habit that had become all too frequent and which tended to help drown the monotony and boredom of their lives. Bluey stood in the doorway and began a jerky dance to the rhythm of the drumbeat.

"Man!" He laughed. "That is some cool beat, I've a good mind to get down there and join in. I might even find a 'good sort' for the night; I could do with a spot of nookie. You booze-soaked bastards are all past it."

Gert snorted. "That wouldn't be a clever thing to do." His German accent, accentuated by the alcohol, made it difficult to understand what he said. He described the events that had occurred with the previous team, of which he had been a part. He thought he was doing Bluey a good turn.

Bluey's comment when he finished was an unequivocal "Bullshit! You're all shit-scared. It's obvious that an animal of some sort got him. I don't go for all that voodoo crap."

The others gathered around and an argument ensued with Bluey getting more derisive and insulting until some of them had to separate him and Gert. But Bluey couldn't let it drop.

After a while Gert jumped up knocking his chair to the floor.

"You're all mouth, Bluey!" He yelled. "If you're so bloody tough vy don't you go down there und join in like you said? I'll give you a hundred bucks to go down there right now. You're full of shit!"

De Wit who was thoroughly sick of all the argument, reached into his wallet, adding "I'll double it."

Bluey looked from one to the other, a look of joyous surprise on his face. "You'll give me two hundred bucks just to walk down to that fuckin' tree?" He asked incredulously. "You're on! Frank can hold the money." He lurched to his feet.

Gert stopped him at the door and told him to wait a moment as he hurried into the store and returned with a hammer and a six-inch nail. "Just to prove you really got there, and didn't fuck up like you usually do, knock this nail into the trunk!" He said. "We'll check it out in the morning."

Already Bluey's mind was leaping ahead to his return and the pleasure he would extract from them all. 'Taking the piss' was his forte.

The room emptied suddenly as they all crowded outside to watch Bluey leave. He walked swiftly waving the hammer as he went. As he disappeared into the trees they could hear his laughter growing fainter with distance.

As Bluey strode along the trail, guided by the moonlight that filtered through the canopy, some of the buoyancy began to leave him. He could hear the drums now, getting louder as he progressed. He plunged on, all the time becoming more aware of the noises of the night; snufflings and movement. Occasionally a screech would send his blood pumping wildly and once there was an unearthly cry as if something was dying painfully. He had not progressed very far when he realised that in spite of all the alcohol he had consumed he was now cold sober. He wished fervently that he had brought a bottle with him. Fifteen minutes had passed when to his surprise he discovered that his muscles were tensed and aching, he made a conscious effort to relax them.

Hurrying now, as much as was possible, he toyed with the idea of going back and making some excuse. But even as the thought crossed his mind he knew that no excuse would save his face, and Bluey, like the Chinese, was big on 'face'. He tried to walk quietly, as if he were hiding from something, but what? His heart was pounding and the sweat of fear coursed down to soak his waistband. Something slithered across the trail ahead of him. He paused, terrified. He hated snakes; even as a boy in the outback he had hated snakes. He moved forward just as a bat swooshed close to his head, he felt his bowels churn and clenched his buttocks fiercely. He could feel a pulse hammering close to his ear and his legs had a liquid feeling. But still he forced himself onwards, glancing fearfully around him as he went. Thorns seemed to reach out to claw him, like fleshless hands.

Suddenly, without warning he broke through into a clearing. It was roughly circular, about fifty yards in diameter, and in the centre stood the Baobab tree. The moon struck it at a sharp angle creating shifting, lacy patterns on the ground and on the tree itself. The sight of it caused Bluey to catch his breath. It was an awesome sight. Massive! The branches reached out as if in agony, a thousand deathlike bony fingers that swayed and clawed at nothing. Over all shone the moon giving a ghostly, ethereal glow that caused the shadows to dance with life, and reflect on the miscellany of objects swaying from braches.

Bluey became aware of his breathing, a rasping tearing noise that sounded unnaturally loud to his fear-enhanced hearing. He tried to still his racing pulse as he sensed a feeling like pounding sea on a rocky shore, somewhere behind his eyes. It took all of his remaining strength and courage to force himself forward, away from the now comforting darkness, into the glare of the clearing. One pace, two paces, the dry grass crunching noisily under his feet. He felt naked and exposed in the bright moonlight. The silence which his appearance evoked did nothing to reassure him.

He moved forward quickly now, his fear spurring him on. He reached the evil-looking tree after what seemed to him to be an eternity. In his haste he tripped over one of the arched roots that rose serpent-like from the ground and measured his length, almost as if in supplication.

With a sobbing cry he forced himself up, gazing about him in terror. His hat hung sideways rakishly over one ear. The insulting tassels drooped over his arm as he raised the nail that was to prove his courage. With urgent strokes he drove the nail home, the noise of the hammering chased the last vestiges of resolve from him and with the sweat from his brow stinging his eyes to near blindness he turned to flee, panic-stricken.

It was at that very moment, as he began to move back to safety and sanity that, so it seemed to Bluey, a large clawing hand snatched at his hat and tore it roughly from his head. All reason fled and there issued from his lips the most terrifying, blood-curling scream that echoed and echoed around the clearing. With a choking sob Bluey fell to the ground.

Back at the camp the men were still clustered outside sipping their drinks and gazing into the darkness where Bluey had disappeared. Hardly a word had been spoken since he had left them. The only break in the silence was when one of them made the necessary motions to fill their glasses. Looking covertly at the others Gert could see that they felt as he did, expectant and guilty. Although they knew what they would suffer when Bluey returned they all wished he were back.

As Gert reached out for his glass the scream reached them, it rang out clearly over the intervening distance, terrible and drawn out, poised, it seemed to go on for an eternity. The glass dropped from Gert's shaking hand and fell to the ground, its precious liquid soaking into the dry earth.

"My God!" said De Wit. "What was that?" No one answered. It was obvious to all that something horrible had happened to Bluey. Every living creature in the jungle seemed to have been struck dumb by that fearful noise that had shattered the night. The men drew closer together gathering comfort from each other. They knew that they ought to do something, but without a word being spoken each one knew that nothing would induce him to leave the security of their camp.

Sober now, cold and fearful, they waited for the dawn, each one racked by his thoughts and his part in the seeming tragedy. Not one of them gave any thought to going to bed.

When dawn eventually overtook the darkness their courage seemed to flow back into their bodies with the warmth of the sun. They prepared to set out to discover what had happened to Bluey.

Threading their way along the trail, with the warm earthy smell of the undergrowth, the singing of the birds and the general feeling of movement and well-being, their spirits rose. Hope began to dispel the gloom – which made the shock more palpable when, on reaching the clearing, they saw Bluey's body.

The Baobab tree stood there; benign now, stripped of its evil aura by the light of day, but still massive and powerful. It seemed to have a strangely satisfied look about it the way it sat heavily on the earth like a well-fed colossus.

De Wit bent to Bluey then recoiled with a gasp. The others followed his gaze to the face. The eyes were open even in death, and mirrored in them was something so horrendous that each of them quickly averted his head. Bluey's face was congested and his mouth seemed all teeth with the lips drawn back in a terrible rictus. His heart had obviously ceased to function after that last soul-searing scream. But what caused it?

It was not until they were straightening the body, in preparation to carrying it back to the camp, that a movement caught Gert's eyes. About five and a half feet up the trunk of the tree was Bluey's hat. It was swaying gently in the breeze, held there by a large nail driven firmly through the long ribbon of yellow cloth that had trailed in mockery from the brim.

En Vacances

Valerie and John sat on their wide veranda gazing over the seemingly endless rows of vines that stretched to the horizon, to where they disappeared over the crown of the hill, their thin naked arms stretched out along the taut wires that supported them, imbuing them with almost religious connotations.

The harvest was in and the resultant wine was already maturing in the oak barrels in the maturation room, where it would stay for the next seven to eighteen months. Harvested in mid March, the crop had been exceptional and would undoubtedly provide some of the best wines ever to be produced in the beautiful Hunter Valley.

They sipped their slightly chilled wine with quiet appreciation; enjoying it and each other's company. It had taken twelve years of hard work and sometimes bitter disappointment, but they had made it at last.

The Hunter Valley, like the Barossa Valley in South Australia, is as well known in London, Paris and New York as it is in Australia for its excellent wines. But it was only the previous year that John and Valerie had managed to reach the peak of their industry – and now they were revelling in their recent successes. This year Australian wines had at last usurped the French wines as the best in the world, and theirs were right up there with the best.

John looked over his shoulder to where the framed certificate of excellence hung and smiled at his wife.

"Well! Val," he said. "We finally made it! The best in the world and money in the bank."

Valerie reached over and took his hand. "Yes John, all those years of trial and error, the scrimping and saving have at last paid off, and we have well over a million bottles in hand. I really think we have earned a long holiday. Where will we go?"

"Yes! I agree about the holiday. The boys can well manage things at this stage and we don't have to do the pruning until June at the earliest, so they won't have too many problems."

"And Babs!" said his wife defensively.

John laughed. "I wasn't forgetting her, Val," he said. "The two boys can organise the labour for the field work and Babs can look after the financial side of things. The boys haven't a clue in that department! I don't know," he said, picking up the threads of the earlier discussion. "We've been to Italy twice on business trips but we haven't seen much of the rest of Europe. How about a visit to England? A quick tour of London, then on to France and Germany. We could combine business with pleasure, check out their wineries and see a few shows – I've always fancied the Follies Berger myself!"

"You've got no chance!" laughed his wife, pulling her hand away, "and no taxi driver would ever find the place if you called it that! You'd probably end up in McDonald's."

They discussed it *ad nauseam* over the following days and finally decided on a date six weeks ahead. They would stay away for six weeks.

The intervening weeks passed quickly with John driving his sons mad, checking the work in hand over and over. They finally told him to clear off and leave them to it or they would move down to Sydney and find work there. Valerie and Babs took numerous shopping trips into Newcastle, buying suitcases and clothes. They even bought clothes for John – which he swore he wouldn't wear. Twice a week Val attended French lessons organised by the University of the Third Age; an organisation that runs a multitude of classes for those who wish to follow up their education in their later years.

She would wake John up in the morning with *"Bonjour monsieur, comment ca va? Que desirezvous?"*

"Oui oui!" He would shout, laughing as he dashed to the toilet.

She would practice her French using him as a sounding board, knowing that he had not a clue what she was saying. He tried hard to match her exuberance but sometimes found it hard going. She bought tapes and played them constantly whilst she did her housework – until John switched over to his favourite country program.

The great day finally arrived and they set out for Newcastle, together with their three children, all of whom had decided to see them off. They caught an Air Pelican flight for the short trip to Sydney. There they transferred to the international terminal for their flight to London. They flew business class where John, who was six foot two inches tall, could appreciate the extra leg room. The plane eventually circled over London, which was bathed in bright sunshine, and they marvelled at the seemingly pulsating green and the colourful patchwork of fields below. They had intended to spend just a week in England but extended their stay by three days in order to see more of the beautiful villages and towns of the South.

Valerie seemed to enjoy every minute but John could sense an air of impatience in her. He understood most of her various moods extremely well and knew something was on her mind. It was not until they arrived at Orly Airport outside Paris that he understood what the problem was. When their turn came to present their passports at immigration he watched as Val handed hers over. With pink cheeks and some hesitation she leaned towards the official and said quietly, *"bonjour monsieur, comment ca va?"* The man smiled with just a hint of sympathy and murmured, *"tres bien, merci madame."* Valerie blushed with pride. From then on it was *'merci'* and *'tres bon'* all the way.

At first John was amused and complimented her on her linguistic skills. But as the days wore on her stumbling attempts at French conversation began to embarrass and annoy him. He soon discovered that almost everyone spoke English far better than Val spoke French, and the whole process seemed an awful waste of time and energy to him.

Two weeks passed before John reached the end of his patience. They were in their hotel room where they had showered and were dressing for dinner when there was a knock on the door. It turned out to be a paper seller with an arm-full of *'Le Monde'*, the local newspaper. John was aware that Val's command of the language was not good enough to allow her to decipher the news in French and for some reason it irritated him. Val smiled happily and handed over the required francs, adding *"bonsoir monsieur, merci beaucoup!"* John watched her searching her vocabulary for additional words as the man edged away. He strode forward, nodded to the Frenchman and closed the door.

"Do you have to keep trying to use that ridiculous language?" he asked crossly. "Half the time they haven't a clue what you're talking about and it wastes a hell of a lot of time! They nearly all speak English and if they want our money I am sure they will make themselves understood!" He stalked off angrily to finish dressing.

Val said nothing, but the smile left her eyes and the constant air of excitement gradually faded. She finished dressing and they made their way to the dining room. Dinner was a quiet affair with Val making no attempt to order her meal in French, as she so often had. She ate without relish and they were soon back in their room where Val said she was tired and would have an early night.

John's anger had long vanished and he lay alongside her unresponsive body wondering how he could bridge the gulf that he had created. The following morning after a bleak breakfast they walked out onto the street and John led her towards one of the large markets where she had loved to barter with the locals, laughing at her own lack of expertise. Today she walked aimlessly hardly speaking, a sad shadow over her face. John asked her if she would like to climb the Eiffel Tower. She agreed without enthusiasm. Hailing a taxi John turned to the driver and without preamble said briefly "Eiffel Tower please!"

The driver nodded and moved off. When they arrived at their destination the taxi driver turned to John and rattled off in French, a conversation that obviously included the price of the fare.

John hesitated for a brief moment, *"merci monsewer, uno minute!"* Then he turned to Val and smiled. "Val," he said. "Would you mind interpreting for me? I don't know what the hell he is saying and you do such a good job." Val hesitated for a moment, then with a smile she leaned forward.

Rocky

‹ᴍ›

Tom, Ken, Charlie, Dennis and Brian sat on the wall outside the school; it seemed somehow natural to be there. Their socks drooped to hang over scuffed boots. It was perhaps an unconscious gesture of rebellion. Their exposed knees bore the scars of a variety of adventures.

Charlie was the only one wearing 'longs'. Not all that long really, his mother having a propensity for cutting off the frayed bottoms and turning them up. At the current stage they were about four inches above the tops of his boots. The rest wore shorts, mostly stained and patched, and they all wore shirts of varying antiquity, mostly minus a button or two, except of course Brian. His shirts were always neat and clean.

Brian was the only son of a single mum. What had happened to his dad nobody bothered to find out. He was a bright lad, always top of the class but a bit of a worry to his pals. Whenever he came to visit any of them he usually brought along his knitting. Tom found it most disconcerting to see him sitting on the settee talking to his mother, knitting away with his 'one plain, one purl' and discussing patterns.

There was a general air of boredom. One week into the school holiday and they were not yet quite used to the independence of an undirected day.

"Wot are we gonna do then?" Charlie asked for the fourth time. Once again he received no reply. There was a general shuffling of feet and a long pause. Ken cleared his throat; his eyes began to light up with the sparkle of inspiration.

"Wot we need is a projick!" He stated triumphantly.

"Wot's a projick then?" Charley asked, with a note of skepticism in his voice.

"Well," said Ken. "It's a job that you do for a week, like, you know, like Mister Millar gives ya in woodwork."

"I don't do woodwork!" Charlie said, skepticism changing to exasperation.

"I think that's a good idea," said Brian, a little too quickly.

"I think it's daft!" From Charlie.

"Well, even if we 'ave this projick we still have to think of summick to do, don't we," Tom muttered.

"Well, my mum wants me to build a hen coop." Suggested Brian hopefully.

"You got no 'ope!" Charlie sneered.

"She's the best cook in the village, and she makes ginger beer."

"Keep it!"

At the mention of food Tom and Ken showed evident signs of interest. Brian pressed his embryonic advantage.

"She's just made a whole bundle of currant buns."

"I'm in!" Said Tom. "Me too!" Echoed Ken.

For two days there was heard the regular thump of hammers and the overloud noise of busy boys. Two large packing cases were nailed together and openings made for the birds. Perches were hung; wire nailed to posts and the job was done.

They sat back on the veranda in the warm sun. Conversation was much restricted due to the abundance of cake and ginger beer that appeared with magical regularity. They surveyed their handiwork with justifiable pride.

Replete at last, they lay around in cosy somnolence with Brian's mother chatting away with a host of seemingly endless trivia. As evening drew near they arose and stretched before ambling off to their homes like amiable puppies; sleepy, with their bellies bulging.

Mrs Eckott sat quietly, a warm smile softening her somewhat severe face. The last echoes of a sun-drenched day disappeared into the night and the racing shadows from the hen coop melded into the general darkness.

Brian's mother went down to the markets the following day and bought eight Rhode Island Reds. Good fat birds renowned as prolific layers and eventually, after they had finished laying, good for the pot. A week went by as everyone waited with bated breath for the great moment. Ten days passed without an egg in sight.

Old Taffy Morgan from up the road was consulted and he advised Brian's mum to get a cockerel to stir them up a bit. Back to the market went Brian and got a very handsome Plymouth Rock, a real mean looking character with a huge comb hanging over one side of his head like a bashed-in shako.

All the gang, Brian's mum and old Taffy, crowded around as Brian showed the cockerel his harem. It showed every sign of rapacious anticipation. Brian went into the cage and set the bird on the perch where it clung eyeing the females with lascivious intent. The crowd stayed on until it got too dark to see, but Rocky, as he had been named, never stirred.

"Reckon it's a poofter," said Charlie.

"You've been done there, Ecky!" Tom muttered.

"Aw, give the poor sod a chance," said Ken. "Per'aps 'e only 'as 'is own breed."

"Perhaps he needs some privacy," murmured Brian's mother doubtfully, thinking of her son's moral welfare. They all packed up and wandered home.

The next day there was still no action and Brian got an earful from his mother for buying a duff bird. Three days passed and Rocky was looking most jaded. It was assumed that he had some sort of disease and the general consensus was that he should be removed before he contaminated the rest. With a deep sigh Brian entered the cage and gave Rocky a gentle push, whereupon he fell flat on his back with its feet up in the air. It was then that everyone could see that his legs were still tied together. Once that was rectified Rocky took a long drink of water, flicked the dirt backwards with his feet and headed pell-mell for the nearest hen, with roars of encouragement from the crowd. A week later the eggs began to flow.

"I told you that was what was needed," Mr Morgan said. "It's like poking a stick up a drain. Ya just need ta get it started!"

The Connoisseur

Tom and Jenny ambled slowly through the market. There were over a hundred stalls selling everything from hand made crafts to old tools and other junk of the sort that Tom had thrown in the dustbin without any consideration of its value. *One man's Junk is another man's treasure*, he thought. The Morisset market had spread out in the last year or so and now covered most of the old showground. A large crowd had gathered at the auctioneering section and Tom could hear the voice of the caller clearly over the noise of the milling crowd that shuffled along, some clutching potted flowers, fresh garden produce or a whole miscellany of bargains.

The sun was warm but not hot enough to force him to wear a hat, which he disliked intensely. Jenny drifted over to where two ladies sat knitting behind a table piled high with the fruits of their labour and began rummaging through a pile of babies' booties, presumably with the intention of purchasing yet another pair for her granddaughter.

He looked around at the heterogeneous crowd appreciating the movement and colour. There were suntanned girls in jeans and summer dresses; children dodging between legs playing tag, or clutching ice creams in grubby fists; fathers raking over old tools in a desultory manner and overall the cries of the vendors and shrill laughter of the kids.

Tom was barely listening to his wife's comments as he reflected on all the work that was lying in wait in the garden, when he finally managed to convince his wife that she had seen enough. He thought of many similar sorties and the cupboards full of objet d'art and crafts that were never used, the potential birthday and Christmas presents lying forgotten on shelves. He sighed with resignation.

Tom noticed a couple as they hove into view; odd looking pair, he thought. The man was heavily built with an over-large belly hanging over his belt. He was dressed in a 'T' shirt and too-small shorts that pinched his fleshy thighs, the waistband hidden from view, and 'thongs' on his feet. Not an unusual sight in itself but what caught his attention was the manner in which the man carried himself. His head was up and he leaned backwards slightly as if to counterbalance the weight of the protuberance at the front. His legs were splayed as he walked, and a picture of Charles Laughton in the film Henry the Eighth came to mind. Tom watched with some amusement. One beefy arm stuck out to the side terminating in a cigarette that was held so far down the fingers that his hand seemed to be clawing at his face whenever he drew on it. The other arm was crooked with the hand resting awkwardly on his paunch, allowing his wife, Tom assumed, to hang on with both hands in a most loving manner.

He had an air of importance, perhaps even some arrogance, as he glanced around the crowd expectantly, as if looking for a friend. His wife was a dowdy little woman, thin and fragile. She wore a tired looking straw hat that had seen better times, but she wore it with a defiant aplomb. Her dress was a size or two too large and drooped sadly from one shoulder, causing the hem to sag down at the side. She looked up at the man with a loving possessiveness, proud yet quizzical. He patted her hand where it lay on his arm and smiled reassuringly. She hunched her shoulders and nudged his arm with her head.

Tom watched as they walked slowly towards him. They seemed to walk on an endless invisible red carpet, deviating neither to the left nor right, pausing only to let the crowd surge past them. When they were almost level with Tom the man spotted a stall on the other side of the aisle and he paused, leaning down to say something to the woman. She nodded enthusiastically and they ambled with quiet majesty over to the table.

The stall was covered with a miscellany of kitchenware, piled up in untidy bundles. Chipped cups without saucers; mismatched plates of all sizes, knives and forks bowls and pots, rolling pins and a whole host of bits and pieces whose use Tom could only wonder at.

The man approached the table with the air of an art collector discovering a long lost Rembrandt. Tom moved closer, his curiosity getting the better of him. The man disengaged himself from the woman and, reaching out a very large hand, picked up one of a set of eight glasses. The glasses were the type mass produced to last a lifetime, heavy, thick-walled, with a Tudor motif cast into the base. He raised the glass up to the light, peered reflectively at it for a moment, nodded sagely, and looked at his wife with conspiratorial reflection. She smiled up at him, her head nodding in affirmation. He raised the glass again, holding it by the base and looked around at the passing crowd. He caught sight of Tom watching him and gave a very knowing, tight-lipped smile. He brought the glass nearer to his ear and gave it a sharp 'flick' with his forefinger. It gave a dull solid 'thunk'. He nodded again with every sign of satisfaction.

"How much do you want for these old glasses?" He asked the stall-keeper, in a very off-hand *I don't really want them voice.*

"Twenty cents each mate," he replied. "That's a dollar sixty in all!"

"A bit pricey isn't it?" He queried, giving his wife a sideways nudge.

"Ah," the stall-keeper sighed. "That's dirt cheap mate." He said, as he picked up one of the glasses and started polishing it with an old rag.

He watched as the big man showed every sign of losing interest. Only Tom saw the wink he gave his wife.

"All right, a dollar forty to you," the stall-keeper agreed hurriedly with a shrug of resignation.

The couple packed their purchase into a string bag and continued their stroll. As they passed Tom he heard the woman say proudly, "Oh, you're a hard man, Fred! Knocking him down like that."

"Well," he replied. "If he don't know the value of his goods he has to expect to be done, don't he!"

Frappin' the Wurzel

It was Friday night and the 'Dog and Duck' was crowded. The rain that lashed the village of Nether Wallop kept the bucolic crowd jostling for a place near the large open fire that warmed the public bar and caused steam to rise from their wet clothes. That same rain flowed in feathered streams from the thatched roofs of the cottages. Falling to the cobbled gullies it terminated at the village pond where it eventually overflowed into a small tributary of the Avon River.

Friday, after work, was when the rural labourers collected their pay, often in the bar itself. An ancient tradition that pleased the publican no end but caused untold domestic dissent.

The bar was crowded and the smoke from cigarettes and pipes hung close to the ceiling, trapped between the heavy timber beams. Corduroy trousers predominated, terminating in heavy boots that clumped noisily on the wooden floor, depositing clods of earth that the boot scraper near the door had failed to remove. The place was warm and noisy and had that comforting smell of spilt beer, burning wood and body odours that reeked of familiarity and tradition.

Young George (pronounced 'Jarge'), was restless. For some years he had held the unchallenged title of village wit and prankster, which in a small place like Nether Wallop was not an easy reputation to attain. His last effort had occurred some weeks previously, when he had 'lifted' a pair of knickers from Widow Morris' clothes-line and a pair of somewhat tatty long-johns from Nutter Jakes' and strung them together from a line that stretched from the Dog and Duck's sign to the only lamppost in the village. It caused quite a stir and boundless hilarity, as people had long suspected that Nutter had acquired the habit of slipping into the widow's back door several times a week in the dead of night.

Had they let it pass few would have been any the wiser, but Nutter raised such a fuss as he reclaimed his property that the ownership was well and truly established. The association was confirmed when he was seen to dash into the widow's cottage, much to her consternation, to return her drawers.

The time before that George had managed some modest success when he had laced the visiting priest's communion wine with vodka and Mrs Prentagast was seen to go round twice. But for a while no opportunity had presented itself and George felt his notoriety fading fast. Into this singularly English scene was injected the alien manifestation of the New World as the door burst open, admitting two very wet Americans. Everybody knew instinctively that was what they were. If you had asked each one how they knew they could not have told you, but some arcane knowledge made identification obvious to all. The rimless glasses of the man; the loud checked trousers that showed below his bright yellow raincoat, and the camera that he carried in one hand.

This impression was confirmed when he smiled at the room in general and said in a deep melodious voice. "Good evening everyone! Not very pleasant weather!"

But even as they responded to his greeting their eyes, slightly bulging, were lasciviously exploring his wife as she struggled out of her coat. She had a pleasant face surrounded by heavy blonde hair and she was what the locals would term 'sonsy'. But what collected their eyes, like iron filings to a magnet, was her truly magnificent breasts. They were large and firm and pointed upwards and outwards. They were moulded into a white skin of fine wool and seemed to dance to some inner rhythm totally divorced from their owner.

Nether Wallop was a pretty little village, but being somewhat off the beaten track usually missed out on the financial benison enjoyed by the sister villages of Upper Wallop and Middle Wallop; this being the case the advent of, what would assumed to be, wealthy Americans was a cause célèbre that brought all conversation in the smoky bar to a halt.

Into this hiatus stepped George, his agile mind questing for opportunities like a ferret down a rabbit hole.

"Good evenun, Zur! Missus!" He said, pushing some of the locals out of the way and ushering the newcomers forward. "Come oover yer to the foier an dry aarf!"

"Make room thar, fellers!" he called, with a wink at the grinning crowd. "Laat these good folks dry aarf a bit."

The locals moved aside to let the newcomers get to the fire.

"That's very kind of you!" Said the American with a grateful smile. "If you wouldn't consider it presumptuous or rude of me I'd like to buy yo'all a drink, but I sure don't want to cause offence."

"No offence taken, zur!" George roared as he fought the rest in their dash to the bar.

The two Americans warmed themselves by the fire for a while then moved over to the bar where they sat on stools and ordered drinks. George joined them.

"Thaank ye fer the ale, zur," he said with a grin. "We'm don' get many tourist yer, we'm bein a bit aarf the beatin traak loik. Where be yoom folks aarf to?"

There was a few seconds silence as the two Americans absorbed the local dialect, broke it down into its component parts and came up with an interpretation.

The woman spoke first. "Well! I guess we don't have any set agenda. We're just travelling around soaking up the local history and getting as involved as we can in the local traditions. You folks sure do have some strange goings-on!"

Her husband gave her a loving smile as he added. "Yeah, Maisie here sure likes to get involved in things, it kinda makes the trip more interesting. She had me dancing all around the streets in that there Floral Dance down there in Cornwall…"

"Yes," Maisie joined in, "and they let me take part in 'Wrapping the Maypole' down in Bishops Waltham, and the fertility festival down in Somerset." George choked on his beer.

"Yes." she continued, "I'll have so much to tell the folks back home in Elmer's Falls. They're just going to be so jealous. Have you got anything scheduled around here? I'd sure like to join in if I can. I just love some of your customs."

"Gee! I think you've done enough, Hon." Her husband murmured. "By the way," he said, turning to George. "My name is Bob Arnold (he pronounced it 'Bub') and this is mah wife Maisie. We're doing the Grand Tour of Europe, but hell, we've spent most of our time in the British Isles. It's so small, and pretty."

George introduced himself. His mind was racing.

It was only three weeks earlier that George and his cronies, all eight of them, had taken part in the local festival of 'Beatin the Burrers'. This was a very old custom going back further than village history recorded, and derived from the days when the entire village would turn out on the annual rabbit hunt. All the men and boys would gather at the sandy loam hill to the south of the village where the young lads would position themselves at the entrances to the rabbit holes and at the command would make a fearful din, bashing pots and pans together and shouting. The men would wait on the other side of the hill with clubs, ready to kill all the rabbits that were thus driven out.

The women's job had been to skin the rabbits and prepare them for the evening celebrations. Roast rabbit and ale followed by energetic dancing and no less energetic frivolities on the common under the trees. It was the highlight of their somewhat insular lives, and tended to initiate the birthing cycle. It was something like the lambing season.

The more modern corollary of 'Beatin the Burrers' was an annual contest, where several teams carried out a stylised dance. Those on the winning team each being presented with a 'Yard of ale', presented by the local taverner.

The dance itself consisted of a team of between eight and twelve men forming a circle with one member in the middle. All were equipped with a stout six foot long stave, corduroy trousers complete with 'nicky tams', pieces of string tied just below the knees – supposedly to stop rats running up their legs and attacking their manhood – leather jerkins and boots. As a fiddler played the men circled the 'victim', swaying forwards and backwards, cracking the staves together over his head. The clumping boots and the clashing of the staves provided a contrapuntal rhythm to the chanting of the participants. The championships were strenuously contested between the villages.

George quested, feverishly sorting through the possibilities.

"Well missus." he said finally, improvising rapidly. "We do 'ave our 'Frappin the Wurzel' cerrymony tomorrer, but I can't say thaat youm be allowed to take part, it bein' for village maidens, loik." He shook his head regretfully. "Not only thaat," he continued, "it be a paart of ower 'arvest festival, celebratin' fertility an' fruitfulness, yoom unnerstand. It wouldn' be fittin fer a leddy loik you."

Maisie's face began to take on the embryonic semblance of understanding acceptance.

"Not thaat you couldn' do it," he added hastily. "It's just thaat thaar be certain things thaat you 'ave to do thaat moit embarrass an outsioder, ye see!"

"Things like what Jarge?" asked Bub, slightly aggressively as he looked at his wife's crestfallen expression. "Ma Maisie sure ain't no prude – as long as things are done tastefully," he added quickly.

"Well." said George, a look of disarming candour on his pink-cheeked country face. "It sort of speaks fer itself, don' it. The maiden chosen fer the 'onner is usually the one with the biggest udders loik. That's the fruitful part ye see. So she 'as to taak part with nothin' on the top loik, ye see!" He watched the American's face carefully, trying to judge his reaction. Wondering how far he could go.

Maisie blushed prettily as she unconsciously pushed her chest out even further, much to the consternation of the bar-room crowd. She looked at her doting husband, shyness and determination fighting for domination. "Well! I wouldn't mind if that is what is expected," she said finally, looking for assurance from her husband, who smiled indulgently and nodded his approval.

"That's if I have the right qualifications," she added with some smugness.

George snorted some of his beer up his nose and doubled up in a paroxysm of coughing. When he finally got his breath he said, with some doubt in his voice. "Well! oi'll go an taak to the committee then to see if it's alright. Weem never ad a furriner taak the part before, oi don' know if they'll agree. Oi wont be laang."

George walked over to the crowd by the fire and after a short whispered conversation drew them all into the empty privacy of the tap room.

"Ar! What do yoom thank of them udders then?" He began with a laugh. There ensued a chorus of 'oohs' and 'aars' all accompanied by broad grins. "Thaars more there than farmer Yager's Jersey!"

"Bah! Oid loik to gaat my 'ands on thaat lot!" From Nutter.

George raised his hand and called for silence. "Ow waad ye really loik ta get yer 'ands on em?" he asked, with a grin. They looked at him, disbelief rampant on their glowing faces.

"Even you couldn't maanage that, Jarge," one muttered regretfully. "But if oi could oi'd never wash me 'ands again." The hubbub started up afresh.

"Whaat's it worth then if oi caald get er to take er top arf an' let ye aal 'ave a look. Oi mioght even toss in a feel fer luck!" he added.

There were laughs of derision and much scoffing at such an impossible feat. But George noticed that Nutter and Bill Bailey were drooling slightly at the thought and several had that vague introspective look of men picturing something beyond possibility.

"Oi'll tell yoom whaat oi'll do," said George. "Oi'll bet yoom aal thaat I can gaat 'er to show yoom 'er boosums. Foive pounds fer a look an' five pound extra fer a feel. Who's aan?"

There were no dissenters. George made his plans, speaking to them for over half an hour. Then he returned to the bar where Maisie waited, becoming increasingly excited at the prospect of baring her breasts and receiving the acclaim that she knew her magnificent appendages deserved.

"Well," began George ruefully. "It weren't aisy but they've agreed. Mostly becaase there baint be no maidin in the village as can match them thar wurzels of yorn. Now oi 'ave to tell ye whaat ye 'ave to do."

"Is that what you call them here? Wurzels? That sure is weird."

"Yeah Jarge, where does that name come from?" said Bub.

"Oh!" said George. "We grows em out on the faarm, they be loik melons, but rounder loik. We grows em fer the cattle. They be rightly called mangle-wurzels. We 'ollers em out on Hallowe'e night an' puts caandles in em. Scares the old dears near to death." He laughed.

Twenty minutes later, with Maisie well rehearsed he returned to his friends to make the final arrangements for the ceremony, set for Saturday night. Maisie and Bob booked into one of the rooms above the bar and went to bed.

All the next day Maisie wore an air of subdued excitement as she rehearsed in her mind the modified Highland Fling that George had told her would be her part in the coming festival.

Just before five-o-clock most of the men of the village could be seen sneaking out of their cottages and the 'Dog and Duck' and heading for the old barn behind the general store where things were still set up very much as they had been for the 'Beatin of the Burrers' festival. During the night bales of straw had been set out for spectators to sit on and bunting had been added to the overhead beams and the small stage set to one side. A small area had been cleared of straw and lamps added for atmosphere.

The word had passed around the village like wildfire, but the women had been banned, much to their annoyance. They were only pacified by George hinting at further opportunities to come.

The doors of the barn were closed and in the gloom the lamps were lit casting dancing shadows over the medieval scene. The barn was fairly crowded with just about every man who could walk - and one who couldn't - fighting for a bale towards the front where Bob had already taken his seat. Out of sight, behind a wall of bales Maisie, now very nervous, glanced around at the men who comprised the dance team. There were now twelve of them, four more having volunteered at the last moment, all grinning with anticipation.

The musicians started up with a lively jig; old Droopy Catchpole with his violin and Smudger Smith on the accordion. There had been little need for rehearsal as everything was virtually as it had been three weeks previously. The jig ended and there was a slight break then the tempo increased as they broke into the opening bars of 'The Farmer's Lad.'

Out from behind the bales of straw trooped a line of dancers, Maisie, having tossed aside her blouse, was in the middle. The men were doing a small skipping step as they pranced towards the clearing and made a circle with Maisie taking up her position in the centre.

She was wearing a long skirt in what might be termed a 'gipsy' style, brightly coloured and tiered, that she had bought in Petticoat Lane a week before. Her small feet were encased in silver sandals and, with some concession to modesty, she had a bright diaphanous scarf around her neck, which did nothing to hide her magnificent breasts that leaped with gay abandon to her dancing. As Boilly Bill remarked, 'they wuz loik fat puppies fightin' over a bone'. The music rose and fell as the dancers moved in and out clashing their staves together and singing. Nutter Jakes' eyes were popping out of his head and twice he dropped his stave. Whacker Jones forgot to move and just stood with his head bouncing up and down as he tried to follow those bouncing orbs. George kicked him hard in the shins and dragged him back into line. The music faltered a couple of times as old Droopy dropped his bow but the tempo was maintained by Smudger, he being half blind was looking around puzzled by the excited buzz that filled the air and the prolonged burst of applause.

All the dancers were sweating profusely having gone through the routine twice at a nod from George. The musicians were heading towards the end for the second time when George stamped his feet on the wooden floor and tossed his stave behind him. In a ragged procession the rest followed looking towards George for a lead.

George signalled Droopy to repeat the song for the third time and waved his hand in a circle to indicate an increase in tempo. The dance became a parody of stamping boots as George improvised and the rest followed. Then, in a darting movement he lurched forward and with the flat of his hand gently rubbed both of Maisie's breasts, then leaped back into the circle with a bland expression on his face. Maisie's eyes opened wide and her steps became ragged, but with a limp smile of acceptance she picked up the steps with increased vigour. One by one the others followed suit. Nutter tried for a second go but was tripped up by George and accidentally stamped on. By now Maisie was showing signs of fatigue, the weight of those ample orbs multiplied half a dozen times by centrifugal force was dragging her shoulders down and perspiration trickled down her lovely body. George signalled the musicians and the pace dropped to a crawl and finally to a close. Everyone clapped and cheered as Maisie hurriedly dashed for her clothes behind the screen.

By eight-o-clock the bar of the 'Dog and Duck' was crowded, and a loud cheer issued forth as Bob led Maisie to a stool at the bar. Safely ensconced and with the 'puppies in their kennels,' according to Boilly Bill, Maisie shyly acknowledged the crowd. Just like Princess Diana, thought George.

Bob smiled at the throng and again called for a round of drinks.

"No zur!" said George, his pockets crammed with pound notes. "It be the custum thaat the 'Maiden of the Village' and 'er consart pays fer nothin on 'er Frappin' night. Everythin is on the 'ouse, zur," he winked to the landlord. "Oi'm doin the 'onners!"

"Well that's very kind of you, Jarge. We appreciate it!" said Bob.

Maisie leaned forward and whispered to George "Did I do alright? I didn't think it would be quite so …strenuous!" she ended lamely.

Bob broke in. "Yeah, and I guess I wasn't prepared for it to be so… fruitful." He murmured with a smile.

George took a long swig of his beer, studying their faces from under his bowed head. He cleared his throat. "I muz say, Missus, thaat were the finest Maiden we 'ave ever 'ad. Everyone says so. You daad roit good." Maisie smiled her thanks and went to speak, but George jumped in quickly. "Thaat were the 'ard part, now there's only the final maarket walk to do!"

"Market walk?" echoed Bob and Maisie together. "What market walk? You never said there was more." Said Bob.

"Oh!" said George. "I must aav fergot. Yoom must do the maarket walk, it's paart of the cerrymony. Yoom just caan't do half of er, it's tradition ye see."

"And just what is this market walk?" asked Bob, with just a hint of exasperation. I think mah Maisie has done enough! I sure didn't think half the village were going to …. to," he stuttered, "… have carnal knowledge of mah wife."

George glanced towards Nutter who was wearing gloves 'to 'old in the feelin'. And felt a slight pang of embarrassment. "Aat's really nothin much, zur!" He said in an aggrieved tone. "All er 'as to do now is to laat the wimmin approve of the 'Maidin', ye see. The men passed er yestidy, now aat's the wimmin's turn."

"And what exactly do I have to do, George?" Maisie asked, curiosity overcoming her concern over Bob's reaction.

"Aw, not much, missus. Ya see on Sundays weem 'ave a small market aan the villige green and aal the villige will be thaar. All ye has to do is walk through showin yer wurzels so thaat the wimmin caan see thaat yoom be well chosen. Some of those who 'aves less thaan yoom has to show their disapproval aan those what thinks yoom won faair aand squaare liok will cheer yoom aan. Thaat's all thar is."

"It sure sounds a bit weird to me' son!" Said Bob, a slight hint of suspicion dawning in his eyes.

Maisie, secure in the certainty of her mammary superiority, could already hear the applause of the throng and she smiled at her husband as she reached for his hand.

"I don't know Bub, it just don't seem right to break with hundreds of years of tradition, does it," she murmured, a soft plea in her voice.

Bob looked from one to the other, his suspicion still in evidence. He looked from George's expression of slightly hurt innocence to his wife's obvious wish to participate. Once again he attributed his suspicions to his long-felt jealousy; a feeling he had fought to suppress for many years. He knew his wife was constant and had never once let him down. He cursed his churlishness.

"I guess you're right Hon, I'm sure sorry I made those comments. If that's what you have to do, go for it."

George, having done the virtually impossible the night before, the crowd in the tap room were not quite so skeptical as they had been. It seemed that nothing that he did would ever surprise them again. "Come aan yoom lot!" he pleaded. "Just two pouns each aan oi'll get 'er to waak through the maarket showin arf 'er wurzels."

"Weeell," said Nutter. "Do weem gaat another feel?"

"Geeze!" muttered George with some exasperation. "Yer felt em last noit. Whaat do yoom expect fer two poun? Oi jest won't do aat agin if thaat's yer attitude," he added, an aggrieved look on his face.

"All-roight thaan," they chorused. "Two poun it is." Each man's eyes jiggled up and down in anticipation.

"Moi missus'll go crackers," chipped in young Frank. "Er aint gaat much aat aall, more loik swollen nipples."

"Ar!" Said Nutter. 'Thaat's better thaan the widder's. Er aas things loik razer strops with cigar butts on the ends."

"Ar! So! The widder is it thaan? Now us knows, don't us!" Shouted old Droopy. Nutter looked from one laughing face to the other. Realisation of his faux pas dawning slowly. Muttering imprecations he turned and stamped out.

As before, word spread quickly and women could be seen standing in their doorways early Sunday morning, talking and laughing with their neighbours as they readied themselves for the market. It would never be so well attended.

"Thaat Jarge is a lad, the things 'e do. Get isself into trouble one day!"

"Oi thaank it's disgustin, oi does. 'E should be locked up. So should 'er."

"Not together I 'opes", yelled Fat Bessie, the publican's wife. "Oi gaat me eye on ee!" They laughed as they all wandered down the cobbled road to the village green.

The market was crowded, but little was being sold. It was half-past-nine when a silence fell on the crowd and all eyes turned up the street to where Bob and Maisie had appeared outside of the 'Dog and Duck'. Maisie wore a pretty summer skirt and blouse and had a large straw bonnet on her head. She thought it would be appropriate for the occasion.

They walked slowly down the street towards the green. Bob held her hand in a most comforting manner and Maisie, her breasts obviously unrestrained, walked proudly, head up. The pummelling inside her blouse gave the impression of a cat fight in a sack. The crowd parted as they approached.

"Well Hon, they're obviously expecting us," she spoke softly out of the corner of her mouth. Bob squeezed her hand.

"Yeah, Hon!" He replied. "I must admit I had my doubts but it seems quite legit. I sure am sorry that I doubted that George fella."

They were almost level with the first stalls when Maisie quickly slipped the buttons of her blouse and removed it, handing it to Bob.

There came a ragged cheer, mostly from the men. Widow Morris bashed Nutter over the head with her handbag. Young Frank's wife went pale and surreptitiously felt her small buds. Frank leaned forward and whispered in her ear "Oi'd rather 'ave yours moi luv." She gave him a grateful smile.

Some of the young girls looked on enviously, and one of the boys whistled and passed rude comments, until his mother clipped him around the ears and hugged him to her ample bosom, so that he could not see.

Maisie looked quite regal as she strolled slowly past the stalls, head high and chest thrusting out.

"Tart!" Yelled the widow. "Yoom look loik a roit tart!"

Bob pressed Maisie's hand. "She's obviously one of those who's got nothing to show," he said.

"Yeah" smiled Maisie, as she strolled along. "It's all part of the ceremony, just as George said."

Everywhere heads turned and smiles blossomed. "My, my, Gertie. I didn't thaank George would really be able to pull thaat one orf," said young Bert's wife. "Very noice, missus!" She called.

Some of the younger women cheered.

Maisie nodded her head with great dignity as she passed.

"Thems looks loik Gunga Din's water saaks!" Cried Nutter's old mother. "Why don yoom go baak were yoom cums from? It aint roit!"

Maisie just smiled, and reaching the end of the stalls, slowly did the return trip.

They walked back up the street with Maisie buttoning up her blouse. "Well," she said. "That wasn't so bad. Obviously most of them approved." She laughed. "Perhaps I will have to come back next year to defend my title."

"I think we might forego that pleasure, Hon," replied Bob.

That night the 'Dog and Duck' was more crowded than ever, with George once again buying the drinks. There was even a scattering of women sitting with their menfolk.

"Ah guess you must have got the local ladies worried," muttered Bob with a laugh.

Several people came over to congratulate Maisie, including two of the women, one of them ending with "If oi 'ad wurzels loik yoom, missus oi'd show moin aarf too." Her words belied the sad look of sympathy that flitted across her face. She glared at George as she passed.

George sat with the two Americans at the bar, revelling in his renewed notoriety. He acknowledged his cronies with a beaming smile and an offer to buy them another beer, which made him more popular than ever.

"I just can't wait till I get back, Bub, and tell everyone how I took part in a ceremony hundreds of years old – and became the Village Maiden. I bet nobody else in the whole of the United States has ever done that. Was I really that good, George?" She said, turning to George.

"Oh yes, missus, yoom were tha best weem ever aad!"

Maisie smiled delightedly. "Gee whiz, I think I could do this for ever," she laughed.

George, with a few drinks under his belt looked from one to the other, speculatively.

"Well…," he said slowly. It just so 'appens thaat weem do 'ave one other cerrymony comin up loik, if yoom could stay another couple of days. It be even better thaan the laast one." His mind was once again well ahead of him.

"Oh," said Maisie doubtfully. "What is that one called?" She asked, her eyes shifting to her husband.

"Well ye see loik, ah, this one be rather speciaal loik. It's called."…, he paused a while. "Ah…, 'Strokin' the Marrer'."

Bob looked at George for a long while, a soft smile playing around his lips. "Not this time, George. Not this time!"

He turned to Maisie. "You did a great job, Hon," he said, putting a loving hand on her cheek. "But it has been a long day and I think it's time for bed." He took her arm and led her to the door as everyone called out their goodnights.

The next morning they arose early, paid their bill and drove out of the village, up the winding road to the top of the hill where Bob stopped the car and got out to look back.

Maisie looked down into the valley where the picturesque village lay, partly in shadow and partly washed by the rising sun. Smoke curled from half a dozen chimneys, but nobody appeared to be out and about.

"Beautiful little place, isn't it, Bub," said Maisie. "Strange people though; quite simple really."

Bob stood beside her, his arm moved to encircle her shoulders as he drew her to him. There was a long pause. "Yes Hon, it sure is a lovely place... But perhaps they're not quite as simple as they seem." He smiled to himself as they got back into the car and drove away.

Authors note;
My apologies to all women – I intended no offence.

Sweet Dreams

Penny was not what you might call a 'morning person', if you know what I mean. Tom, of course, didn't know that when he married her. Not that it would have made a lot of difference, the power of the loins being what it is, you understand. Whereas Tom could sleep for as little as four hours in any one night, and still be able to jump out of bed with a song on his lips, Pen. needed to enter each day like a rebirth. She emerged from darkness to light with the utmost reluctance and indignation.

Often in those first years Tom was reminded of an old English public school tradition, where any boy not wishing to speak, or to be spoken to, in the morning would wear his hat and it was forbidden for anyone to speak to him until he removed it. Tom was tempted to suggest she do the same, but she was seldom sufficiently compos mentis at that time of the day to allow him to broach the subject, at least, not until she had supped a cup of tea and stamped around for a while, by which time he had forgotten the problem.

As the years passed a happy mean was arrived at. Tom learned to curb his early morning exuberance and Pen. managed to evolve a reasonably noncommittal grunt. This state of affairs continued with varying degrees of success until Pen. entered her U.S.E. - Ultra Sensitive Era.

What provoked it is somewhat uncertain. Perhaps it was some degree of stress from the university course that she was taking. The subject matter was frighteningly onerous and left little time for relaxation. She arose early and drove for two hours to get to the uni. and had a two hour drive back again at night. Whatever the cause, the effect was that she began to require absolute stillness from Tom in order to be able to sleep.

Now it so happened that Tom was a restless sleeper. He tossed and turned and would often go down to his study in the middle of the night and work for a while. Prior to the U.S.E. Pen. had learned to live with that, but this was something different. The first time that he became aware of it was on a Sunday night. Pen. had been working on an essay all weekend and around eight-o-clock had fallen asleep in the armchair. She awoke somewhat disgruntled about nine-thirty, turned down the television so low that Tom could hardly hear it, and stamped off to bed.

Tom recognised the signs immediately, of course, and knew that if he turned up the TV to a point where he could hear what the characters were saying, there would be ructions. He also knew that if he delayed going to bed until she was asleep his arrival would awaken her with dire results. So with some reluctance he joined her, knowing that retiring that early meant that he would lie awake for several hours.

Pen. turned on her side and curled up in a foetal position, her back to Tom. Soon a gentle sawing, like the purr of a contented cat, filled the room. Tom lay on his back with his hands behind his head and gazed into the darkness as the outline of the window, between the open curtains, crept from the night and the weak gibbous moon patterned the sill. His foot touched hers and he felt a slight twitch; he slowly eased his foot away. A few minutes passed and his arms began to ache; with infinite care he began to lower them.

"Do you have to keep fidgeting?" She snapped peevishly.

"Sorry love!" Tom replied, taking the opportunity to scratch his ear as he turned on his side. He thought about a story he was writing and a rather neat phrase came to mind. He knew that if he did not write it down he would forget it. He began to reach slowly for the pad and pencil on the bedside table, but a sharp backwards kick caused him to abandon the idea. He strove desperately to etch the magical words on his brain.

The minutes ticked by and Penny's breathing resumed a regular even pattern. Tom's nose began to itch. He twitched it a few times but the itch continued. Then he began to feel the increasing discomfort of his pyjamas where they bunched in his groin, the side of his foot developed a tic and the large toe on his right foot went into spasm.

He concentrated on the ray of light from the moon and focused all his attention on its silver path. He dwelt on the silver glow of the window's edge and the dancing shadows from the trees outside. The rest of the toes on his right foot joined their mate and the pain became unbearable. He stretched his leg and turned his toes up, breaking the spasm.

"For God's sake, are you going to keep this up all night? I've got to get up early in the morning. Can't you have any consideration at all?"

As she was now obviously awake Tom again took the opportunity to quickly rub his nose, scratch his head, readjust his pyjamas and scratch his groin. He settled himself comfortably, taking care to get everything just right. His wife grumbled and groaned and moved further over to her side of the bed.

"Sorry love! Goodnight"

One knee was pressing too heavily on the other; he slid it off.

"Humph!"

A while later a cold draft began to impinge on his left shoulder where his wife had pulled the covers over to her side. The chill began to creep down his back.

'Tomorrow,' he thought, 'I'll cut the lawns and clean the car. No! Perhaps I'll drive around to the car wash, it's only five dollars.'

His shoulder was getting quite frozen and he began to shiver slightly. He gently edged towards his wife, hoping to get some exiguous warmth. There was a break in the even tempo of her breathing. He stopped edging and tried to push the covers down with his chin. This being fraught with danger he desisted.

'To convert sixty degrees Celsius into Fahrenheit you multiply it by nine. That makes it five hundred and forty, and then divide it by five. Five's into five hundred and forty equals one hundred and eight. Then you add thirty-two making it one hundred and forty degrees.'

Tom felt a strong discomfort in his bladder. 'Damn it!' He knew he should have gone before he came to bed. Two cups of tea whilst watching the play on the A.B.C. always caused a problem. He had been told a dozen times that tea was a diuretic. He closed his eyes and willed himself to sleep. The discomfort increased to an insistent urgency. His body began to sweat and he found his hands and toes clenching and unclenching. He fought the agony for a few more minutes then succumbed to the inevitable and hot footed it to the bathroom.

He returned a while later to an empty bed; his wife had fled to the spare room.

Crawling back into her warm spot, Tom wrapped the bedclothes tightly around him, scratched his toe, rubbed his skull, tweaked his nose, adjusted his pyjamas, hoisted his privates and gave out an enormous sigh of contentment.

Bazaruto

Bazaruto lies twenty-four kilometers off the Mozambique coast opposite Inhassoro in the Mozambique Channel, and is the northern-most island in the Bazaruto Archipelago. On a clear day you can see the white cliff-like sand dunes reflecting in the sun low down on the horizon. At night the Don Carlos lighthouse winks its light to warn off seafarers and at the same time beckons like a siren, with soft seduction, the diver to its underwater paradise.

The sea around the islands teems with a vast variety of fish, Barracuda, Kingfish, Queenfish, Bream, Bonito, Marlin, Swordfish and a whole host of others which, together with the coral, golden sands and coconut palms, must make this God's own special reserve.

We had sailed up from Durban and because of the lack of any sheltered bay or harbour on Bazaruto had decided to leave the boat at Inhassoro on the Mozambique coast and hire one of the many Arab traders to take us over in his dhow. The owner of the boat was a very thin, deeply tanned individual. He had a remarkably wrinkled, hawk-like face topped with an exceedingly grimy turban; however he was pleasant enough and directed his crew to help us load our gear and stow it below the shallow deck where it was relatively dry.

There was very little wind but the dhow made good headway under the huge sail, hoisted by means of a thirty foot bamboo balancing gaff and augmented by an ancient Seagull outboard that spluttered into unconsciousness every fifteen minutes or so. The removal of its single spark plug and the vigorous application of a wire brush constantly resuscitated the motor. We saw many dolphins and the occasional shark as they drifted through the wave tops. Once a turtle of magnificent proportions, about four-foot across the back, plodded along with massive dignity and purpose.

Soon the yellow-white sand spit that marks the southern point of the island became visible, but it seemed ages before we finally closed it and headed towards a suitable beach. Unloading and setting up camp took a couple of hours but we had plenty of willing help from the local native village and we were soon relaxing with a 'still cool' drink. We waved the dhow away with the skipper's promise to return for us a month later.

A quick foray into the near reef produced our evening meal of fried sea bream and parrot-fish – the first of a long line of delicious meals to come. That evening we retired early, tired but unbelievably happy with the stars clear and bold overhead and the sound of the restless surf in our ears. Carried on the gentle breeze we could hear singing coming from the native village. We seemed a long way from all the concerns of the modern world.

The next morning we were up early, winkled out of our sleeping bags by the urge to get started. Soon the aroma of bacon, eggs, coffee and toast was drifting across from the cooking area which we had arranged in the lee of a huge sand dune. The entire camp site was criss-crossed with the tracks of hundreds of crabs that had checked out the remnants of our previous night's dinner.

Our first real dive was on the first of three reefs which was about fifty yards off the shore. The water was only about twenty feet deep but teemed with fish and glowed with brilliant colours from the coral. We spent two days on this reef improving our breathing prior to trying the further reefs. I was diving into a deep channel when several huge parrot fish drifted by. They must have weighed at least fifty pounds and were about three feet deep and five feet long. I had no idea they grew that large. Thinking of the delight of the villagers when I presented it to them I lined up on the largest and fired just behind the head. The slender stainless steel spear hit a scale and fell off with the pierced scale attached. The fish glared at me with one eye and continued on its way totally unconcerned. Our spear guns were state of the art stainless steel air guns with a supposed killing range of thirty feet. The cylinder was fully pumped up using a hand pump and the action of reloading with a special tool strapped to the wrist reset the firing piston; but it couldn't penetrate the armour plating of that giant fish. We hired one of the village lads to do the washing-up and to keep the camp clean and tidy and through him arranged for some of the locals to take us in their canoes to the furthest reefs which were three hundred and five hundred yards out and to follow us whilst we fished. They were not all that keen until we dived overboard and reappeared some thirty seconds later with two 10lb parrot fish. We showed them how to unscrew the spear points and to remove the fish for us. They were happy to do so as we gave them all the catch, apart from those we wanted, for them to dry and sell to the Arab traders with enough left over to feed the entire village.

The beauty of the underwater scene revitalised our senses and amazed us anew with its vividness and variety. The fluttering brightness of the multicolored boxfish with their tiny wings and horned head entranced us, as did the puppy-like devotion of the porcupine fish that followed us up and down the reef with enormous eyes peering shyly at us from under long eyelashes. We had our scuba tanks but had no compressor for refills so we only used them for one deep dive on the outer reef and all our fishing was done using snorkels and spear guns.

For the first few days we fished at depths of twenty to thirty feet but were soon diving to eighty feet as our lungs became used to the depth and our breathing improved.

Near the reefs the ebb and flow of the surf was quite strong and wet suits and gloves were a necessity to avoid injury, even then we did sustain various cuts and the occasional jab from sea urchins which necessitated the use of our extensive medical chest on our return. The villagers, having been informed by our helper of the wonders of our medicine, were soon queuing up for treatment. One old man came with an enormously swollen foot from a shark bite. We drained it and dusted it with an antiseptic powder and bandaged it. Strangely he recovered. We had babies with constipation and diarrhea, septic fingers and burns. These we treated with no problem. One woman had a mass of septic holes all over her arm. The chief explained that it was from a particular species of fly that lay eggs in clothing and that when hatched penetrate the skin and grow into large grub-like creatures. We made up a bread poultice and covered it with ointment and slapped it on her arm. She gave an outraged howl, much to the merriment of her peers, apparently it was too hot. The chief said it had healed – but I doubt it. My pal had to be restrained from major surgery.

One morning, having cleaned and checked our 'bang sticks' (a short stainless steel tube with a spring loaded plunger, into which you loaded a bullet or shot gun cartridge) and cartridges, which were sealed with nail varnish, we headed seaward of the outer reef. Here the seabed dropped away sharply until it disappeared into a deep blue haze. We were after sharks. After half an hour trying to get them to attack we finally took to spear guns and shot a few twenty-pounders which we left on the seabed. Twice the sharks snatched fish off our spears but as soon as we swam towards them they would dash off out of range. My pal gave up and soon speared a seven-foot moray eel, which promptly drew back into a deep cleft bending the spear into a figure eight. It took him nearly half an hour to finally dislodge it after hitting it several times with his 'bang stick'.

I was wearing cotton gloves, the kind that has a backing of hard bead-like knobs as protection. Fishing at sixty feet I shot a thirty pound kingfish that took off like a rocket, I was dragged along behind it. In its dashing and threshing it dragged the line over my gloves and around several rocks. I tried to free my hands in order to cut the line but the beads held the line tight. Running out of air I began to panic; it was then that my partner, Roy, seeing my predicament swam over and severed the line allowing me to make for the surface to get some air. Having recovered I retrieved my spear-gun – and the fish. It proved yet again that you should never dive alone. I remember well the old adage, 'dive alone, die alone'. I never wore that type of glove again.

We finally discovered that the only way to get a shark to attack was to swim on the surface and splash our flippers; that seemed to attract them. Perhaps they thought we were injured fish. We could then dive at them and hit them on the bony part of the head. The first time I did this I was totally unprepared for the consequences.

To every action there is an equal and opposite reaction and I was forced backwards and my legs flew up behind the shark I was lucky not to shoot myself in the foot. The explosion made my head ring and I watched, with some confusion, the shark spiral away to land on a coral ledge where we attached a line so that the locals could tow it to shore. We discovered that when they circled, humped their back and oscillated from side to side, they were preparing to attack. The greatest lesson we learned however was that sharks can be very unpredictable.

We drifted back to shore fishing as we went with the boat following us. We had fished for four hours and our catch consisted of 220 lb. of fish, one seven-foot eel, two eight foot sharks, two lobsters and two leopard cowries.

The following day we decided to visit the lighthouse. The thought of a cool drink and a cold shower had become an obsession, so we started off along the beach chasing crabs and collecting shells as we went. About thirty minutes later an opening through the trees gave us a clear view of our objective and our spirits quailed at the sight of the extremely steep and very long climb up. The going was soft sand for the most part and there was very little shade. By the time we reached the base of the building we badly needed that drink.

The keeper was a most pleasant old man who chatted away about the time he had spent in Johannesburg years previously and he seemed pleased to have somebody from the outside world to talk to. He gave us wonderfully cold water and we climbed the circular stairway to the top of the lighthouse where we had a magnificent view of the whole island and could revel in the cool breeze. Before we left we took turns standing in an ancient chipped bath letting the cold water shower wash away the salt and sand of the previous week. It felt glorious. The water was pumped up from a well at the base of the lighthouse and there appeared to be no shortage. We took leave of our host and arranged for members of his family to visit us the next day to collect some fish.

The pattern was set for the following weeks which passed all too quickly. We would fish one of the reefs for three or four hours and have our main meal just before the sun had set. After dinner we had a few games of 'max and jacks' and enjoyed good conversation, which seemed to get better depending on the number of mugs of coffee and brandy that we had. The way we solved the world's problems should have earned us a Nobel Peace Prize. From 10am to 3pm the heat was so intense that we usually covered our noses with a thick coating of sunscreen and stayed virtually under water with only our faces exposed. Our rendering of Delta Dawn at the top of our lungs brought the local children, who gazed at us from the safety of the coconut palms with wonder on their faces.

One day whilst fishing on the second reef a large turtle passed me. Thinking to do the villagers a great favour I grabbed it by the back of its shell and guided it ashore where the locals were overjoyed. Two days later whilst walking past their village I saw the unfortunate turtle still alive, lying on its back with its flippers waving slowly and its head hanging down. I called the chief and complained at the treatment but he looked at me confused. To him it was sensible to keep it alive and fresh until they wanted to eat it. I never caught them another.

Inevitably the end of our holiday arrived and we took to the water for the last time. We did not know exactly when the dhow would arrive, or even if it would. We had made arrangements with the boatman before we left, but I think we hoped that he would forget.

We started fishing early in order to fill up our small fridge, choosing for our hunting ground a large rocky mound near the sand spit at the southern end. We watched, prodded and generally soaked up the environment like sponge memory banks. I was drifting along with the current in about twenty-foot of water looking for likely lobster spots when a huge shadow moved across my vision. It was a marbled stingray about six foot across the wings and about twelve-foot long. It had an eight-inch razor-sharp spike protruding from near the base of its tail and it was moving slowly with a gentle flying motion. I moved above it and slightly behind and managed to get off a shot from about six foot, which hit just forward of the eyes. It took off at great speed and I lunged for the surface to get a breath of air and managed to get my flippers up to increase the drag. Each time I got to the surface I yelled for assistance and with the help of Roy and two natives managed to tie it to the boat where it was towed ashore. The ray tipped the scales at 240lbs and had to be cut into pieces to weigh as our scales did not read that high. In the stomach were a number of trigger-fish and a whole miscellany of other small fry. The locals were overjoyed at this unexpected delicacy and were still celebrating when the dhow was spotted rounding the headland.

By the time it had reached the beach we had packed our gear and the locals helped us load it all on board and waved us off. Quite a wind blew up on the way back and spray blew across the deck. We were alright in our wet suits but the crew were soaked even though huddled under canvass sheets. It took nearly three hours to reach Inhassoro where we transferred us and our gear to the boat in the dark.

That night we slept like the dead and early next morning weighed anchor and headed up to the Seychelles. It was a delightful trip. The people were a happy lot and always helpful.

As we headed north we promised ourselves that we would do it all again sometime; but we never did. Bazaruto, that pristine island paradise was discovered by entrepreneurs some years later and lost its virginity to a mass of holiday makers; the lighthouse lost its lovable, garrulous keeper and was automated; several dive centres were established and the villagers displaced.

The Octopus

I had been in the Fleet Air Arm branch of the Royal Navy for five years when I was sent to Malta, to be stationed at Kalafrana, once a seaplane base, on Burzibugia Bay. The place consisted of workshops, accommodation and a slipway for launching the seaplanes; which at that time were Otters and Walruses. The station was located on the edge of the bay with Joe's Bar as the focal point of the curved road that framed the bay. Further round, on the opposite side to the station, was Jimmy Dowdel's bar. Jimmy was of indeterminate age; certainly over sixty; a large man with fat stubby fingers that caressed the old piano keys with just a hint of magic. His theme song, which he sang with gusto was "Fish gotta swim all over the place; birds gotta fly or fall flat on their face." Jimmy's was the favourite haunt of the Med Fleet most weekend evenings and often through the week. The rest of our off-time was spent in Joe's, mostly playing 'sevens, fourteens and twenty-one's'. A debilitating game where all participants threw dice and the one who threw seven named the drink – usually some ferocious concoction, the one who threw six had to drink it and twelve paid for it. Joe was happy and usually we were so bombed out we didn't care. The front doorstep greeted you with 'Welcome'; the spelling of which was dictated by some illiterate matelot deep in his cups and which was too expensive to dig up.

Our accommodation fronted the beach where the golden sands swept down to what was once the clearest azure blue sea in the world, where you could see the sea creatures crawling on the sea bed twenty feet below or watch, the fish chasing each other through the multi coloured rocks Anchored off the beach, some fifty yards out in the deeper water was a raft from which we could dive or sunbake in the fairly constant warm sunshine that pierced the endless blue of the sky. Most weekends were spent with my pal Pip, wandering through the backstreets of Valetta where we would inevitably end up in Captain Caruana's Bar for a few beers prior to sampling the hearty delights of Chez Vancy's restaurant, where, if you managed to eat a full serving you could order more on the house.

One afternoon we had been delighted to have been approached by Jack Hawkins and his leading lady, Dulcie Gray, who were in Malta together with Michael Denison and John Gregson working on the film, Angels One Five. We were wearing our uniforms and without hesitation the pair had walked over and asked if they could join us. Naturally we were delighted to have their company. They refused to let us buy a drink and entertained us with stories appertaining to their profession all afternoon. Of course we made the most of this encounter and bragged outrageously about 'Our Friends, Jack and Dulcie', for weeks. Our surrogate fame was enhanced in timely fashion some weeks later - just as our flame was becoming somewhat dimmed – by a chance encounter with Alec Guinness, who was starring in the Malta Story with Jack Hawkins, although the latter was not there at that time. He proved to be another charming man who sat with us for short time. This caused some strain on relationships with our shipmates.

A mile or so around the coast from Burzibugia was Octopus Creek, a sharp cleft in the rocky cliff with a path leading down to a small beach. The name was apt as many octopuses bred there, sometimes growing to an impressive size. I had discovered that one of our messmen had a great liking for the cephalopod and that his wife skinned them and made a delicious, highly spiced dish, a bowl of which was always passed on to me. I would take my spear-gun and mask and flippers and search the turbulent seabed until I discovered one lurking in a rocky cave, or if I was lucky swimming freely. They were not easy to spot as they had chameleon-like attributes and altered their colours to match the surroundings. If they were anchored to a rock or in a cave I had to persuade them to leave and become unattached before catching them as they were extremely difficult to prise from the rocks – and I only had one deep breath. One day I had managed to spear quite a large specimen; it proved to be over twelve feet in length across the spread tentacles. It became something of a talking point – in which I gloried, of course. That night I was in Jimmy Dowdel's bar with a young lady, Joanna. We were sitting on stools at the bar sipping John Collins' when the door crashed open and a crowd of officers barged in, already well stoked. They ordered drinks and then sat on the floor facing the door, obviously expecting someone. They wore various comic headdresses and were in a festive mood. A short while later the door opened and in walked Prince Phillip. I recalled that at that time he was the skipper of HMS Magpie, which was on a visit to Malta. He looked at his officers, who were all salaaming, muttered something that sounded like, 'silly buggers', and walked up to the bar where he ordered a pink gin.

Joanna, seeing the prince was electrified. She was bouncing on the balls of her feet as she pushed past me to get closer to the great man and was obviously dying to speak to him. I attempted to calm her down but to no avail; nothing would stop her. She finally reached his side and in an embarrassingly gushing rush declaimed.

"Excuse me, Sir," there was a slight pause, "Tom caught the biggest octopus they have ever seen in Octopus Creek." Then spreading her arms as wide as they would go she continued. "It had testicles bigger than this!"

There was a dead silence for a moment as this incredible declaration sank in. Then the Prince turned to her and without a change of expression said, "How remarkable." At which the entire crowd burst into loud and prolonged laughter. Joanna, realising her gaff, blushed a deep crimson and dashed from the room. I finished my drink relishing the piquancy of the tale and then followed her.

Holy Smokers

My pal Mike and I had bought a boat in England and set off to sail around the world. The boat was a thirty foot long Golden Hind; designed by Maurice Griffiths. She was a sturdy little boat with a raised deck and twin bilge keels. It took us about a year to reach the Galapagos Islands where we arrived one Sunday morning to a mixed reception. (See "The Fifinella Log" by the same author). Never arrive in a foreign port on a Saturday or Sunday you will incur double fees and usually somewhat grumpy officials who were looking forward to a quiet weekend

Due to the arguments and hassles we were not too impressed, however we did meet a charming woman and her daughter who had just completed a mammoth walk up the length of the Andes – all with the intent of using their experiences in a book entitled, "Eight feet in the Andes". The eight feet being hers, her daughter's and Juana, the mule's. Dervla Murphy was a remarkable woman having cycled and walked through some of the most intimidating areas of the world collecting material for her numerous books. Her daughter, Rachel, seemed to be more like her friend and appeared to be almost as erudite as her mother. We invited them to join us for breakfast on our boat the following morning, expecting them to call out and wait for us to bring them out in the dinghy. However at 7am there was a loud knocking on the hull, they had swum out. She had one bad experience whilst on the island, after leaving the post office she discovered that she had left her purse containing her money and airline tickets on the counter;

when she returned they had gone, which left them in an unhappy predicament.

We left Galapagos with a fitful breeze on our beam and headed for the Marqueses Islands in French Polynesia; some three thousand miles away. Hiscock, in one of his books states that everyone should experience the doldrums to learn patience. It had the opposite effect on me. Days drifting with not a breath of wind, in forty degrees of heat proved soul destroying. Every time we saw a slight ruffle on the water from a vagrant breeze we jumped into the dinghy and towed the boat into its path to find inevitably that it vanished before we reached it.

Forty-six days later we sailed into Nuka Hive with only two litres of water remaining in a container and virtually hallucinating for a cold beer.

Having completed the meager formalities we wandered up to the only store we could find and to our delight and surprise they had cold beer. They were fairly large bottles and when we had finished guzzling the contents we took the bottles back hoping for a refund but we were informed that the beer came from Tahiti and if we wanted a refund on the bottles we would have to take them there. As that was our next port of call we collected every bottle we could find on the beach and those tossed into the bushes until we had filled the bilge and every spare space. The locals looked on in amazement. We rattled our way past the Tuamotu Archipelago and on to Tahiti.

On entering Papeete we were cleared by the various officials and finally found a cheap spot to tie up. The first thing I did was to take some of the bottles to the store to see if they would pay the deposit. The woman in the shop explained that the bottles with red labels had been discontinued and were worth nothing but she would take all those with blue labels. Discovering that the brewery was no great distance from the harbour I walked into reception and requested a hundred blue labels. We soaked off the red and attached the blue and finally ended up with nearly thirty dollars.

The following day, having settled in we decided that a walk would do us a world of good. Walking along the path that edged the harbour we saw a rather flamboyant character coming towards us. He appeared to be about mid-forty years old and by his clothes we assumed he was American. He wore Bermudan shorts and a shirt of bright colours and sandals. As he came up to us he smiled and asked where we were from. I explained that we were on a sailboat.

"Holy smokers", he replied, "you guys are lucky, I'm sleeping in a hire car. The hotels here are the most expensive in the world. Everything is twice the price it is at home."

"That'll be America, won't it?" I asked.

"Holy smokers, no", He exclaimed. "I'm Canadian. You can call an American, Canadian, But don't ever call a Canadian, American," He commented with a laugh.

I couldn't tell the difference.

He went on to explain that he had lived with his wife of some twenty-five years, and had two children. Apparently he had a plumbing business. One day he had a heart attack that put him in hospital for a week or so – this event had obviously scared him a great deal and caused him to re-evaluate his life and his options. The family were well catered for and he could see no point in working himself to death just to make more money. After some deliberations he had packed a few necessities into mainly plastic bags and set off for the Polynesian Islands where he hoped to get to some sparsely inhabited island where, I assumed, he would become titular king of the island. We later discovered that he had acquired a copy of a large tome on Polynesian languages, apparently written by monks of some obscure calling.

I deliberated a while and then suggested that if he wanted to join us on our boat he could have the use of the fore cabin until we departed. He was overjoyed and we spent the rest of the afternoon sight seeing around the island where we collected various fruits prior to returning the car to the hire company.

"Smokers", as we chose to call him – although his real name was Roy – was soon settled in the fore cabin and made himself at home. The following morning I called to Mike in the other bunk, to ask whose turn was it to make the tea; a ritual performed every morning.

"Yours!"

Our morning tea was something special. It was well brewed with two sugars and condensed milk. I called to Smokers to ask if he would like a cup.

"Holy smokers, no. I'll just have organic water."

I looked askance at Mike and mouthed, "What's organic water?" His shrug indicated that he had no idea. So I pumped it up out of the tank that had been filled in Nuka Hive – it was not very wholesome. I took it in to Smokers to find him rummaging in one of those doctors cases, the ones that looks like a carpet bag with drawers and containers. He was swallowing pills by the handful.

"Hell, Smokers, what are all those for?" I asked.

He explained that 'these' were vitamins, 'these' were for his heart; 'these' were enzymes for indigestion.

I quietly suggested that perhaps he wouldn't have indigestion if he didn't take so many pills. He just smiled wryly.

Further down the line of boats was a sixty foot charter boat with about a dozen adventurers aboard and every day we would have a steady parade of visitors who welcomed a cup of tea and an opportunity to voice their discontent over the skipper of the boat and his arbitrary decisions and bad attitude. It was a most unhappy crew who had paid $12,000 each for a two year world cruise that had apparently gone wrong. On a boat you have to make absolutely sure that all those on board are compatible because in the close confines all irritations are magnified ten-fold. At least we allowed them to get their problems off their chests. Luckily they insisted on taking us out for meals and naturally we did not object too much.

A few days later Smokers expressed his gratitude for letting him stay on our boat and insisted that we join him in the local club for a 'boogie'. I asked Mike what a boogie was but he was just as puzzled as I was. That night we 'tarted up' as best we could with our salt stained meagre wardrobes and rowed ashore where Smokers led the way through various back streets to the club of his choice; The Piano Bar.

When we entered we were quite bedazzled by the throng of beautiful women. Even making allowances for our months at sea we could see they were somewhat above the ordinary. Behind the bar was a very tall, large breasted wench dressed in a full wedding outfit complete with veil. We were gobsmacked. We sat on stools at the bar and ordered drinks. Within seconds we had women either side of us stroking our knees and asking if we would buy them a drink – of course we complied. Ten minutes later Mike leaned over to me and indicated with a wink that he was going outside with his woman; I wished him luck. A few minutes later he was back red in the face and spluttering. "They're all blokes, every one of them," he snarled. "This is the only Gay bar in Tahiti." Needless to say I roared with laughter at his discomfort.

Even with our ardour dampened it still proved to be a lively and interesting evening. Through an archway we could see into another room which had one wall completely covered with mirrors. The patrons danced to loud music whilst looking into the mirrors and dancing with their image.

About one-o-clock in the morning we were treated to a strip show with a difference. In Polynesia in general, if a woman gives birth to three or four boys in a row the next baby born may be regarded as a boy, regardless of its sex. He is dressed as a girl and does all the housework as a normal woman does. The child is known as a Mahu and is not necessarily a homosexual, although this is often the case. This one took a fancy to Smokers, who by now was fast asleep standing up against the archway with a beer glass still gripped in his hand. Having removed his jock-strap revealing his manhood, the Mahu sidled up to Smokers and drew it across his upper lip. Smokers awoke with a start and taking in the scene at a glance gave him a shove that sent him reeling and let out a roar. "Get that gaddam thing away from me!" He yelled, pushing it away and spitting profusely.

We were still laughing as we paddled back to the boat. As we climbed back on board Smokers was busy stuffing more pills into his mouth and entreating us to go Boogie again.

We declined his kind offer.

A week later we prepared to head off to Morea, an island about thirty miles to the west of Tahiti. Smokers had made arrangements with the skipper of a fishing vessel who was heading to his fishing grounds about a hundred miles south of Tahiti. He agreed to drop Smokers off on a small island that, he assured him, had water and a small tribe of natives living on the south side. We watched as he climbed aboard with his plastic bags, Polynesian dictionary and his bag of pills and waved until he was well out to sea.

One day I hope to go and look for him.

Spider Loves Me

It was a chilly, wet evening and the rain that slanted down, driven by a strong wind, lashed against the shop windows, making the displays inside look as if they were melting. Windscreen wipers threw spray backwards to catch the bright lights, enshrouding the long line of slowly moving cars in a tunnelled halo.

Pedestrians hurried along with their heads down trying to keep under awnings and away from kerbs where water, thrown up by passing traffic, saturated anyone foolish enough to pass within range.

Life for most of those out and about or just scurrying home was without doubt somewhat uncomfortable at that moment, but most had somewhere to go. Perhaps a warm home and a loving family, or just a lonely flat lacking a few amenities, but a base, a place of refuge; a cat for companionship or a television to help pass that time between dinner and bedtime. There may indeed have been those who would rather be out that night walking the streets in preference to going home to controversy and argument.

In a city there are a whole range of scenarios ranging from the excesses of the rich and famous, the deliriously happy, the sad and lonely. There are those who attack life with joy in their hearts and boundless *joie de vivre* and those who, in despair beyond our imaginings, court death as a blessed release.

There are also those who live in a world thrust upon them by circumstance or abstruse happenstance, where their first step has been the wrong one on a path that leads to a cry for help in a back alley, or huddled foetus-like in a syringe-strewn room in a corner of a derelict house.

To the average person the intense emotive nuances that flutter butterfly-like across the minds of those in this shadow world are barely understandable, their origins lost in personal suffering. We cannot understand the motivations of these wind-blown minds because we have not been there. We have not had to grasp at the crumbs of life, like a drunk searching for a chink of light to stop him spinning.

Joan Southcott from Social Welfare and her companion Jack, a captain in the Salvation Army, picked their way carefully between the piles of rubbish, tin cans, old car tyres and other less salubrious detritus that littered the foul-smelling alley. Their torches searched the darker spaces, looking for a bundle of rags that could possibly harbour one of humanity's discards whose grasp on life was, at best, tenuous.

Joan held a handkerchief to her nose as she led Jack through a doorless gap into a derelict building that she had discovered earlier in the day. It had been vacant then, but several signs had lead her to believe that someone needing help could be using the place at night.

Their torch lights flickered over discarded syringes and blood-soaked tissues that littered the floor, together with piles of faeces and empty cans and bottles. They made their way across the room to another opening that led deeper into the bowels of misery to where they could see the fitful, flickering loom, of a small candle in an island of isolation. As they neared, a woman, roused by their footsteps, rose heavily from a badly stained and torn mattress that was spread out on the floor in a corner. A wooden box with a makeshift shelf held the candle that was standing in a tin lid. Some attempt at privacy was evident in the torn curtain that had been nailed between what looked like a broken basket-ball stand and the wall, and a few odds and ends of clothing drooped from nails.

They studied the woman as she rose. She was very much over-weight and the puerperal bulge that distended her midriff did nothing to ameliorate that fact. Her head was shaven, creating a bluish tinge to her scalp. A line of small earrings adorned both ears and the tank-top that she wore was rucked up over her pregnancy showing a navel that had turned almost inside out, displaying a further ring that stuck out painfully from an infected mound.

She faced them somewhat defiantly, her gross body sagging with neglect and despair. One small eye peered over her fat cheeks whilst the other gleamed dimly from a bruised and swollen eye socket.

"Hello! I'm Joan and this is Jack!" The welfare worker said with a smile. She held out her hand to the young woman. She showed no signs of revulsion or distaste as she took the hand that was offered in return.

"Is there anything we can do to help you?" she added.

The young woman made no immediate reply.

"Will you tell us your name? We have nothing to do with the police. I'm from welfare and Jack is from the Salvation Army. We would like to help you!" She persisted.

Finally. "We don't need no help! I've got my own man who looks after us!" She said with a slight hint of belligerence – and something else. Joan tried to place it. Was it pride?

"Are you on drugs?" She asked kindly; surreptitiously scanning the girl's arms for needle tracks.

"No I'm not!" Her voice lifted. "Me and Spider don't do that stuff!"

"Will you tell us your name? Just your Christian name will do!" She asked again with a smile.

The girl looked at them and they could see the battle within as her defence mechanism searched for any possible repercussions.

"Desiré!" she said at last. "There's a dash above the 'e'!" she added reluctantly.

"Ok! Desiré, that's a lovely name. When is the baby due?" She asked, glancing at the exposed swelling.

Desiré smoothed her stomach gently and tried without success to stretch her clothing down to partly cover it. "Only about four weeks now!" she said proudly.

"And could I ask how you got the black eye?" Jack inquired solicitously.

Desiré glanced towards the door. "I deserved it." she muttered. "Spider did it, but it was my fault. He brought a bloke round for me, but I didn't want to do it. He was drunk and threw up all over the bed," she indicated a stain on the corner of the mattress. "And I was frightened it would hurt the baby." she added.

"Does Spider often bring men home for you?" Joan asked.

"No!" she snapped, seemingly outraged at the thought. "Only when we ain't got no money for food. He usually manages to find something."

Just then soft footsteps could be heard approaching. They turned towards the sound.

Spider turned into the room and saw them standing there. He paused for a moment, hands in pockets and a cigarette hanging loosely from his lips.

"What do ya want then with my woman? Oo are you? Some of them fuckin' do-gooders then ay?" Never 'ere when ya want em, an' always pokin' their noses inta where they're not wanted."

He turned to Desiré. "I don't want you 'aving fuck-all to do with 'em. You 'ear me? I don't want you 'aving nothin' to do with 'em, or I'll close that other eye. Do ya 'ear me?" His voice rose.

"It wasn't my fault Spider, they just came in. I didn't ask them to come. Honest!" Her voice had a pleading note.

"No! It wasn't her fault, Spider," said Jack. "We're just going around seeing if we can help people. Desiré will be needing help soon. She obviously can't have her baby here, can she?"

They watched as the truth penetrated his brain. He had obviously not thought that far ahead.

Joan studied him, wondering what attracted the girl to him. He was short in stature and very thin and wiry. His head was shaved to match Desiré's, and the gaunt outlines of his skull appeared skeletal in the dim light. He wore a string vest and torn jeans, through which could be seen his bony knees. He stood with his legs wide apart and his skinny arms stuck out from his body in what he obviously thought was a macho stance. All the joints that were visible were covered with spider-web tattoos, whence he had obviously acquired his name. Joan and Jack were neither shocked nor surprised; they had met many similar kids before who hid their vulnerability behind a cloak of toughness gleaned from third-rate movies.

Spider turned away, not wanting to get into a discussion that would expose his shortcomings or crack the shell of his assumed persona. As he swaggered away he lit another cigarette from the stub of the last.

"You can fuck off and don't come back!" He glanced towards Desiré, "and you make sure they're not 'ear when I get back or you'll be sorry." He walked out of the room, flicking the stub of his cigarette towards them.

"Listen Desiré," began Jack, "we can get you into a hostel until you have your baby. They will look after you and make sure that the baby is ok. Once you have had the baby it will be up to you. What do you say?"

"Yes! It will be far more hygienic and you will be well looked after," added Joan.

"I ain't leavin' Spider. He looks after me and he's getting us a better place of our own soon."

Joan tried another tack. "Why did you leave home in the first place, dear? Can't you go back and let your family look after you? What happened?"

"Me dad's dead, he died three years ago. He was 'ardly in his grave when me mum picked up another feller in a bar. He was always sticking his hand up my dress when me mum wasn't around. Even when she did see him she only laughed. Then he started coming into my bedroom, and me mum couldn't care less. He was a bastard! So I left, and me mum was pleased to see me go. I hate her!" She paused, then continued. "I was in a bad way, everybody just used me, and then Spider came along and took me in."

"That's a very sad story, Desiré. We hear stories like that every day. But we can start you off again on the right track. You know the sort of work we do, we can make your life so much easier, you must be aware that we have helped many others." Joan stopped talking and studied the girl. Her look of defiance had returned and she stood a little taller.

"Why won't you leave him, Desiré?" Jack tried again. He looked at the girl with compassion, then he glanced around that awful room. "What makes you stay with him?" He asked.

Desiré looked at them. Her face mobile in the light of the guttering candle. Defiance chased other emotions across her face. Not a lot of hope, but a wistful pride. A pride of having her own man? A pride of being cared for? She held their gaze for a while and then lowered her head and they could just make out the quiet whisper.

"Spider loves me!"

The Contest

Just as the lights turned to amber the sleek new Jaguar came to a smooth halt. The middle-aged man behind the wheel leaned back comfortably in his seat and smiled. He was smartly dressed and his pencil thin moustache and chequered 'cheese-cutter' denoted him as something of a dandy.

He looked to his left as a battered old V.W. Beetle pulled up alongside. Its missing engine cover seemed to give the impression that the car was possibly a 'hot rod'. He glanced disdainfully at the other driver, a tall, thin, pimply youth with the unkempt, careless look of the times, sitting hunched over the wheel.

The young lad glanced sideways at the Jag. and its driver and grinned slowly. A wolfish, hungry look full of teeth. He revved his engine twice; it gave the deep throaty roar of a punctured exhaust.

The driver of the Jag. surreptitiously slipped his car into second gear, his foot resting lightly on the accelerator. He slowly increased the revs. Once again he glanced furtively at the young boy alongside him and inadvertently locked eyes. The lad smiled briefly and again revved his engine as he edged closer to the line. The older man gritted his teeth and his hands gripped the steering wheel tighter.

The lights changed to green and the Jag. leaped forward across the intersection, the back of the car fishtailing slightly as the rear wheels fought for traction. Blue smoke erupted from the tyres. The young lad, the smile still evident on his pimply face, put his car into gear and slowly drove off.

Maria

⚜

Jesse, Frank, Mel and Bob were lying on their towels in the hot sun like a line of sausages on a barbecue grill. The beach at Bondi was crowded with near naked bodies – all denying the Almighty his dues on that Sunday afternoon. The shrill voices of children seemed muted by the short distance to where they played in the sand at the water's edge; their sand filled bathers sagging to the back of their knees and a heavy coating of sunscreen glistening on their faces. Occasionally the intrusive note of a whistle, followed by a shouted warning from a lifeguard, acquainted them with the information that someone on the surf line was drifting out of the patrolled area.

Jesse reached over his head to grope in his bag for his sun-glasses; Frank watched covertly from under his wide-brimmed straw hat as a girl lying a few feet away slipped her bikini bra straps off her shoulders and holding her bra to her chest lowered herself onto her towel. He could see the rounded curve of her breast and just a hint of a nipple.

He saw her watching him and let his eyes drift away, as if he wasn't really all that interested. She wasn't fooled.

The four of them, all in their late twenties, had been meeting almost every weekend since leaving school. An extra dimension had been added a few months previously when Jesse's uncle had died and left him a somewhat ramshackle beach house down the coast just short of Kiama. Once a month they would stack their wagons with beer and supplies and take off on a Friday evening after work, returning late Sunday. Sometimes they would make a concerted effort for a few hours to carry out critical repairs, but generally they would play cards, swim, sunbathe and generally 'chill out', as Frank put it. Their conversation, as usual was desultory, consisting mostly of comment on their jobs, any attractive women in the vicinity, and good humoured jibing.

"Well?" said Mel, directing his query at Jesse. "Who is she then, and what are we missing?"

The others looked up expectantly, smiles on their faces. Everybody knew what Mel was alluding to. The previous weekend Jesse had excused himself from the gang declaring that he was going down to the cottage. 'And no! He didn't need their company.' After endless ribbing Jesse had finally conceded that he was, indeed, taking a woman with him. Of course they had all courted women from time to time, but seldom had they been brought into the group. On the few occasions when this had occurred the whole atmosphere had subtly altered, there appeared to be a necessity to fill in those quiet gaps in their conversation. Their normal concourse seemed suspended, as if an alien had suddenly appeared in their midst. The women had tried hard to break through the ring of association that had bound them for so many years, but had invariably left with the firm conviction that any further relationship would be one-on-one.

"Right then! Who is she and when are we going to meet her?" Bob laughed as he posed the question. As the rest joined, in Jesse rose slowly to his feet, a comfortable grin on his face, and ambled off to the water's edge without speaking.

"Hell! It must be serious," muttered Mel as he gazed after the retreating figure, his eyes squinting against the sun. "We can usually bank on a blow-for-blow account of his conquests. He's never been this secretive!"

"He's never had many blows," laughed Frank.

"Don't worry about it," muttered Bob drowsily. "She'll be a no-tit intellectual, ban-the-bomb, tarot-reading, crystal gazing freak with the sex drive of a sloth!"

"Yeah! Hair swagged back, horn-rimmed glasses and no make-up!"

"More likely a bone-bag full of neuroses!"

The comments continued, each voice vying for the most outrageous remark.

The object of Frank's earlier scrutiny raised herself off her towel and glared at the three men. She gave a snort of disgust and flopped back onto her towel – but not before Frank had got a good look at her exposed breasts.

All three of them were well aware of Jesse's penchant for the somewhat 'different' in femininity; definitely the intellectual type. Never in all the time that they had known Jesse had any of them felt the slightest feelings of attraction to the women of his choice, which was a constant source of surprise. Jesse, as they all agreed, was the best looking of the group. He was slightly above average height, olive skinned, with just a hint of the Italian. His thick black hair and large brown eyes made him stand out in any crowd. He was never short of money and was well on his way to taking over his family's fruit and vegetable empire. Women threw themselves at him, hoping to gain a foothold in his affections. When they fell short they occasionally landed on one of the lesser mortals, in the shape of his friends - they had no jealousy and accepted the crumbs with gratitude. They were aware that Jesse's parents had strong views on who he should marry. In the Old Italian manner they had chosen the daughter of his father's partner in order to further the family interest. None of them had seen her yet as she was still at university.

Jesse emerged from the sea, water glistening on his well muscled body. He stamped up the sand to where they lay and stood over each protesting body in turn and shook off the excess water. He flopped down onto his towel.

"I'll tell you what I'll do!" He began with a grin. "Next Friday we'll all go down to the cottage and I'll bring Maria down for the weekend." He smiled to himself, knowing very well what they thought of his choice of women.

"Maria is it? I can't wait!" muttered Frank.

The following Friday evening, after work, Frank, Mel and Bob loaded the provisions into Frank's wagon and headed down to the cottage. Jesse was to follow them later, having arranged to pick up Maria from her flat.

By the time Jesse and Maria arrived, the rest had already changed into their loafing clothes and were well into their third beer. As the car drew up in front of the balcony they all wandered down to the car, ostensively to help Jesse with his luggage, but in reality to meet the new girlfriend. She had been the sole subject of their conversation all evening. They all had a mental picture of her firmly etched in their mind, mostly uncomplimentary. In fact so sure were they of their mental imagery that their surprise was complete and obvious to the gorgeous apparition who swung her long legs out of the car and walked confidently towards them.

Jesse introduced her to the gang, noting with an inward smile, their surprise. Maria had jet black hair, a high forehead and large sparkling eyes. She wore no make-up, nor did she need any. Her lips were full and luscious and when she smiled her large teeth were white and even. She wore a low-cut shirt that was tied into a loose bow just above her almond-shaped navel. Her denim shorts flared out from a tiny waist to capture an almost perfect derrière that swayed provocatively as she walked. Jesse and Maria made a most attractive duo. She strode towards them, swinging a wide brimmed hat, confident, poised and friendly.

She laughed and chatted to them constantly as she moved around the house familiarising herself with the layout. She took a proffered beer and dropped into a wicker chair beside them, drinking out of the bottle as they were, and each one of them felt as if they had known her all their life. She slotted into their tight-knit exclusivity as if the opening had always been there waiting for her.

Maria finished her beer just as the sun finally set and the warm glow of sunset pervaded the balcony. Kicking off her sandals she ran lightly down the steps and headed for the surf some fifty metres away.

"Who's for a swim then? Last one in cooks the dinner."

The four men looked at each other. Frank raised his arms in a gesture of surrender and leaped to his feet. Mel and Bob followed. Without pausing Maria ran into the water and plunged into the surf, the others followed. Jesse, now laughing out loud, wandered into the tiny kitchen to start preparing the evening meal.

Ten minutes later Maria led them back up the beach, singing a slightly bawdy rugby song as they went, their soggy clothes sagging around them. – none of them made any attempt to forge ahead of the woman. By the time they had showered and changed Jesse had set out a huge bowl of spaghetti bolognaise, after which Maria brought out a cake, 'by way of celebration'. The conversation flowed smoothly, punctuated by humorous stories and much laughter; most of the attention was focussed on Maria. Sometime after midnight, when they retired to their own sleeping area, each one of them had a deep hunger.

The following morning after breakfast, Bob wandered down to the local news agency to buy a paper. It was about a fifteen minute walk and when he returned the place seemed deserted so he made a cup of coffee and settled down to catch up on the news, assuming that they had all gone for a walk. After a few minutes the rising sun shining in his eyes caused him to turn his chair around so that he faced inward. He sipped his coffee as he searched for the rugby results in the sports pages. He was deeply engrossed when a movement caught his eye over the top of the page. He raised his head slightly and felt the hot blood suffuse his face. In his confusion he buried his head in the newspaper, a whole gamut of emotions sweeping over him. Slowly, inevitably he again glanced up to where he could see into the room where Maria's reflection shone out from the full length mirror in her bedroom. She had obviously showered and was in the act of leaning forward to drop her full breasts into her brassiere, her back was turned slightly away from him. He stared, mesmerised. A terrible guilt swept over him and he knew he should not be watching. A whole kaleidoscope of emotions exploded in his mind, but try as he might he could not drag his eyes away.

He felt a deep disquiet, knowing that the group as a whole had an unwritten code that prohibited any encroachment into the private arrangements of any one of the gang. Apart from which, Bob was naturally morally correct, possibly to the point of being on the verge of slightly prudish. He hated himself for watching but felt totally incapable of foregoing the pleasure that the sight of her naked body provided. A deep blush suffused his face and his mouth hung open as if to enable him to drag more air into his lungs to compensate for his ragged breathing. He saw her pause and dragged his eyes up to where her face was reflected in the mirror and immediately locked eyes with her.

Maria disappeared from view for a moment and reappeared wrapping a dressing gown around her. She walked out on to the balcony to where Bob sat, his face still red, showing his deep embarrassment. She pushed his paper aside and crouched down in front of him, taking his hands in hers.

"Don't be embarrassed, Bob," she said with a smile. "I'm not. I'm quite used to walking around in the nude – you should try it. It is perfectly natural."

Bob looked into her lovely eyes and was lost. "I am so sorry, Maria," he murmured. "I really didn't mean to watch you; but you are so beautiful I couldn't take my eyes off you."

She smiled. "So you think I am beautiful, do you?"

"You don't need me to tell you that," he replied, as he laid aside his newspaper. "But it is not just that, Maria," he continued. "You are the first woman who has ever fitted so completely and naturally into our group. It is quite magical the way you have cast your spell over all of us in such a short time." Involuntarily his eyes dropped to the front of her gown, which had fallen open, partly exposing her breasts. A deep blush once again began to suffuse his cheeks. He reached out for her hands as he arose, drawing her up with him. He pulled a chair away from the table and turned it around for her. She sat facing him. He seemed unaware that he had not relinquished her hands. He seemed to draw strength from her as slowly began, with Maria's prompting, to talk about his life. It seemed to Maria to be a cathartic necessity for him.

"I was the only son of a Presbyterian minister who was determined that I would follow him into the ministry. My father was blinkered in his outlook and had a tendency to see the world in black and white, with no half-tones. He believed that his religion was a serious thing that humour and laughter would dilute. Early in their marriage my mother, I am told, had been an ebullient, bubbly person with strong religious ties. She was convinced that she could charm her somewhat dour husband and show him the joyous side of God, but his stronger will had prevailed and as the years passed she had grown morose with the constant crushing of her personality.

When I arrived on the scene she withdrew into her own world; just her and me. The more she doted on her baby the more resentful my father became. He vented his spleen on me whenever my mother was not around. I grew to fear and despise him. Once, when I was twelve years old, my father burst into my bedroom uninvited and surprised me in, what my father called, 'self abuse'. He called it a despicable and totally degrading pastime that showed a basic flaw in my character. I of course was not so naive as to believe that. I was well aware that other boys in my peer group did the same thing. Indeed, if they were to be believed they 'did it' at every possible opportunity. It was not so much the action itself that bothered me, it was fact that my father had seen me do it, and that he took every opportunity to obliquely allude to it. Of course had my mother known of the situation she could have easily put my mind at rest but, like most boys, I could never talk about that subject. The singular effect that this had on me, at that tender stage of my life, was to associate sex with feelings of guilt and inadequacy. My pubescent fumblings with the opposite sex invariably ended in embarrassment which progressively erected a mental barrier that was difficult to surmount.

Maria watched him as he seemed to struggle for words. He looked at the beautiful woman sitting beside him and saw only warmth and sympathy mirrored in her eyes as he hesitantly continued to tell her his innermost fears and frustrations, a subject that he had found impossible to broach with anybody before.

"My love life," he continued, "if that's what you could call it, hasn't been all that great. I think the main reason is that I have never found any woman who was sympathetic enough, or had the patience to help me get over the barrier. In fact," he murmured with some self-conscious surprise, "I have never found a woman before with whom I would dream of sharing my problem. With you it is different." He paused and looked at her, his need mirrored in every feature. "I haven't been able to think of anything else since I first set eyes on you. It is very painful."

Maria was a warm hearted woman. It could not be said that she was immoral, perhaps not even amoral. She was a woman who enjoyed life to the full and supped of its pleasures with joy and without remorse. Maria would do nobody any ill and generally left the world a better place for her passing. She metaphorically clasped mankind to her ample bosom, not because she needed to, or craved the transient pleasures of random sex. Seeing the naked desire in Bob's eyes she felt a general compassion for his need. She knew that she was beautiful and had more than her fair share of sexual attraction, but she was not promiscuous in the sense of 'any time; any place; with anyone.' She was generally philanthropic with eclectic rather than catholic tastes. Her buoyant and restless nature normally precluded long relationships, and sex had no deep religious significance to her. It was a pleasure to be enjoyed selectively.

"Very painful is it, Bob? Is there anything I can do to help?"

His eyes pleaded with her.

Rising to her feet she took Bob's hands in hers and gently led him into the bedroom. With the powerful all-consuming need satiated and the long sought release a reality, remorse seeped in to fill the void. He hurried to the shower in an attempt to wash away his guilt; to expiate what he considered his violation of trust. He ran the water hot enough to create pain in self-indulgent flagellation, but even as he recognised his perfidy he admitted to himself that were the opportunity to afford itself again in the future he would be powerless to resist. He changed into his bathers and joined the rest on the beach.

The following weekend Bob excused himself from joining the rest of the gang on the grounds of pressure of work. The other three, together with Maria all piled into Frank's wagon and headed for the cottage. Only Maria knew the real reason why Bob had chosen not to go, and she was saddened. Jesse rummaged under the house and dragged out a length of fishing net about twenty feet long and six feet high, which they strung between two trees. With Jesse and Maria on one side and Frank and Mel on the other they spent an energetic hour playing their own version of volley-ball. Sweaty and exhausted they all retired to the balcony for a beer and then wandered down to the water's edge for a swim.

As the afternoon shadows lengthened and the sun began to droop Mel stretched himself out in the shade of a tree, and with his hat over his eyes promptly fell asleep. Jesse had gone up to the house to rinse the salt off his body under the outside shower and to change into his shorts. Maria was splashing in the shallow water at the edge of the surf line. Frank could see down the beach to where the curved bay terminated in a rocky cliff, past which he could see more sand shining in the distance. He rose and brushed off the sand that clung to his damp shorts and decided to take a walk to discover what lay behind the point. In all the time they had been coming down to the cottage not one of them had ventured that far. He started off along the beach.

Maria watched Frank walking along the water's edge and being of an inquisitive nature decided to follow to see what was beyond the rocks for herself. Frank had reached the point before Maria caught up and they rounded it together. The view before them brought a cry of joy from Maria and they ran into the tiny bay like children, laughing with pleasure. The bay was only about one hundred and fifty feet across and was totally enclosed on the landward side with a tall vertical cliff topped with coarse brush. At the bottom was a jumble of rocks and a small sea-carved cave with a deep layer of sand lining the floor. The silver sand, the cave and the rocks that reflected the azure blue from the sea made a picture-book scene that enchanted them. They raced around investigating every nook, from the crustaceans on the rocks to the coolness of the cave. They were soon hot and sweaty and Frank flopped down on the sand, his chest heaving. He heard Maria give a wild laugh and he sat up and watched as she slipped out of her bathers and with a joyful shout dashed into the water.

Frank watched as she cavorted in the shallow surf, the spray did nothing to hide her from his gaze. He rose and wandered down to the water's edge, his probing eyes never left her as she dived repeatedly into the waves. "Come on Frank!" she called, "It's skinny-dip time. Come on in." Frank needed no further urging and was soon alongside her.

Ten minutes later, refreshed and pleasantly cool they left the water and walked up towards the cave. Maria, ahead, bent to pick up her bathers and Frank suddenly felt a painful surge of adrenaline, which quickly migrated to his loins. He hurriedly tried to get into his shorts an activity that was becoming increasingly difficult. He glanced up to where Maria stood; his panic and red face had set her to laughing at his discomfiture. Noting her reaction he grinned boldly and made no move to cover himself up. I'm sorry Maria, he laughed there seems to be nothing I can do about it. I don't think I have ever known a woman who has had this effect on me so quickly, I'll ache for a week."

"That bad, is it?"

"Worse!"

"Then don't bother about those, Frank," she said with a gentle, sympathetic smile as she walked into the cave and spread her costume on the sand.

Frank had little of the reticence of Bob, nor did he have the same feelings of guilt that had assailed his friend. Presented with an offer that he had no intention of refusing he did not hesitate.

Afterwards they once again plunged into the water, dressed and made their way back to the now empty beach to find the others.

Maria did not join them the following weekend and they missed her more than they could express. Jesse explained to them that she had phoned telling him that she had 'a bit of a cold' and would join them the following Friday. Much of the gaiety and suppressed excitement that had been a constant undercurrent when she was near was missing, and strive as they might they could not recapture the previous ambience. For some arcane reason her name was not mentioned, as if each one of them held it in sacred trust. Each had periods of introspection whilst he recaptured in his mind Maria's vivacity; her laughter and her charm. They drank more than they usually did and their private thoughts left long gaps in the conversation. For the first time since they had been using the cottage, the weekend was not a success. Without any consultation they collected their gear and left after a silent lunch on the Sunday. Mel, who lived close to Maria, promised Jesse that he would call at her flat the following day to see how she was and take her a bunch of flowers from all of them.

Mel was physically the least attractive of the group. He was thin faced and his fair hair was already prematurely cringing away from his high brow. He was a gentle soul who constantly wore a frown of concern and slight confusion. Shy and hesitant in his manner his sensitivity had evoked in his companions, and indeed most of his acquaintances, feelings of protection that tended to cocoon his life. Mel was possibly the most intelligent and academically qualified of the group, and indeed was still studying at the University of Sydney for a Masters Degree in physics. As with many shy people he had feelings of great compassion and an infinite capacity for love. He, above all the others, was totally entranced by Maria, a particularly unique experience, believing as he did that he had absolutely nothing to offer a woman of her beauty and charm; failing to realise that it was that very aura of helplessness and compassion that was attractiveness in itself.

Monday arrived at last, as it is wont to do, and Mel awoke late and bleary eyed after a restless night. He had a cold shower in an attempt to shock his system into normality and skipped breakfast in his dash to the uni. He was unsettled and could not concentrate. He had a constant air of subdued excitement at the thought of meeting Maria that evening.

He called a local florist and arranged a large bunch of flowers, detailing specifically exactly what was to be included and how it was to be presented. He had lunch at the uni. Mel was too nervous to feel hungry and made do with a toasted cheese sandwich and was soon soaking in the bath. He took his time, shaving carefully and dressing himself in his best casual clothes.

He was not consciously going courting, his own lack of self esteem would have prohibited that, but he did want to create the best image that was possible with the tools the Almighty had given him, desperately wanting her to like him – he dismissed any further hopes. As Maria's flat was only a block from his he decided to walk, but soon regretted that decision, the flowers cradled in his arms earning him several wolf whistles.

He discovered the block of flats standing in its own landscaped grounds, together with two other blocks, and entered the vestibule. The names of the occupants were displayed under plastic on a board near the lift and he was soon standing outside her door on the third floor. He knocked on the door and waited. Finally it opened and the object of his unbidden thoughts stood before him. She had obviously hurried from the shower, her gown was loosely wrapped around her and she was still busy drying her luscious hair as she welcomed him.

"Mel! What a lovely surprise." She drew him into the room, closing the door behind him. "And you have brought flowers! They're so beautiful," she cried joyously as she planted a kiss on his burning cheek. Mel stammered an almost inaudible greeting and dropped the flowers. He hurried to pick them up and his head collided with Maria's as she did the same. Rising quickly he almost buried his face in her cleavage. Dropping the flowers once again he stood looking at her, mute with embarrassment. Maria laughed as she ruefully rubbed her forehead and holding up her hand she told him to stay where he was and she would pick up the flowers, most of which had tumbled from their wrapping.

Maria watched him as he muttered his apologies and her heart went out to him. She knew instinctively that he loved her and had a good idea of the thoughts of inadequacy that tortured him. She did not see before her a slightly built man with receding hair, his gaucheness and haunted eyes. She saw a gentle man; a man easily hurt; a man capable of deep understanding and sensitivity. She unconsciously noted the care he had taken with his appearance and knew the reason for it. Taking his hand she led him into the room.

They sat in the lounge sipping the coffee that Maria had made, together with slices of home-made cake. Maria leaned back against the arm of the settee, her legs tucked under her, whilst Mel sat stiffly upright at the far end of the same seat, his cup balanced awkwardly on his thin knees. Maria wanted to put him at his ease, to make him feel comfortable with her. She suspected that he had never had a close relationship with a woman and could see that he felt awkward and out of his depth. All her life she had experienced the admiration of boys and men. She easily dismissed flattery and the obvious attempts at seduction. With sexual predators she could be ruthless. The key to her affections was not wealth nor was it crude masochism. Like most women she revelled in her beauty and in the effect it had on the opposite sex. She enjoyed lovemaking as an animal passion but enjoyed even more the pleasure that she brought to her unions for those who truly needed her. She felt a deep compassion for this ingenuous and naive man beside her.

"You're still at uni, aren't you, Mel?" She could see him gathering his thoughts. He began to appear more comfortable as he moved into known territory.

"Yes," he replied with just a hint of animation. "I take my finals for my Masters next month. My thesis was completed three weeks ago."

"You'll be pleased when that's over. Have you got a job fixed up yet?"

Mel leaned forward and relaxed visibly. "I have had offers from several companies but as yet I have made no final decision. I think that the CSIRO has a lot to offer by way of an interesting position, but it's early days yet," he smiled.

"And what exactly does physics entail? I have a general idea, but what role do you play?" she asked with every sign of interest.

Mel warmed to the subject and for the next half an hour talked animatedly. He obviously loved his chosen career. In spite of her previous misgivings Maria found herself quite interested. He had moved closer to her whilst emphasising a point and all the hesitancy had disappeared. He was knowledgeable and erudite and gave the subject life and originality. He accepted Maria's offer of another cup of coffee, revelling in the growing, and unexpected closeness of their relationship.

Maria smiled at him. "Does a woman fit into this ambition of yours? Life can't be all work, you know. Have you got anyone special in mind?" She saw the look of intense longing on his face and could have bitten her tongue. "I mean, you must have had girlfriends along the way."

His hand went up to the side of his face, to where she had kissed him, and a slow blush began to suffuse his cheeks. "I've never seemed to have time for girls," he murmured. "I went straight to uni. from school and I have been there ever since. There always seems to be a lot to do. You know."

She reached out and took his hand. "Are you embarrassed because I kissed you?" she asked gently. "You are still touching your cheek. You must have been kissed before!"

Mel watched her for a while; he seemed to be groping for words. He looked at her and was reassured, seeing only kindness and sympathy.

"The only woman who ever kissed me was my mother," he said finally. "And she died when I was eighteen. She saw me off to university and was gone when I got back. She meant more to me than my education and I should have been there." His voice had dropped to a whisper. "My father was killed in a car accident when I most needed him. These things, and others, tend to take away any pretext of continuity in my life; I have been made constantly aware of the frailty and tenuousness of our contentment; always conscious that the loosening of a nut on life's machine can overnight alter the mechanics of our lives. I think that the whole tenor of our existence, our happiness, is always subjective and tenuous."

"That's very sad Mel, I know. Unfortunately many people have had to suffer in similar ways, but that doesn't mean that everything we love is going to be taken from us. We may have to start again, building up trust and affections like links in a chain of events that as a whole make up our lives." She watched as Mel seemed to disintegrate into a picture of dejection, his Adam's apple working as if to pump up tears. She put her arm across his shoulders. He continued with quiet intensity.

"For a long time now I have closed off personal relationships, apart from the gang, and tried to look inwards, relying on my imagination to replace reality, it's safer. Nothing can inhibit your mind from its free flight. The deepest dungeon, the heaviest chains can't stop me from flying above the clouds, or exploring the depths of the ocean." He looked up momentarily into Maria's eyes, and blushingly continued, "or the innermost privacy of your body and brain. In my imagination I can smell, hold, taste and love you and nothing can stop me. The mind is a marvellous thing; it has its own virtual reality. It's an escape mechanism and a gateway to dreams. It eludes the mundane, dispels boredom and manipulates a loved one like a puppet. It can enhance a subject or bend it to your will. It is not subject to refusal. It spans the oceans and negates time. It circumvents pain and falsehood and can make the object of your dreams attainable."

Mel began to shudder, as if his burden was too heavy for him to bear. He held her hand in a fierce grip as if he would never let go and a tear trickled down his cheek. His shoulders shook and his face bore a look of fathomless need.

Maria rested her cheek against his and their tears mingled. A while later she took his hand and led him into her bedroom.

The following weekend the whole gang, including Maria, drove down to the cottage. They all realised now that the group would never be complete without her. They laughed louder and showed off, each vying for her attention. Each one covertly watched the others to ensure that their association with Maria had not been compromised. Over the following weeks each one contrived to be alone with her for a few rapturous moments, and each one was over solicitous to Jesse in an attempt to compensate for their discreditable behaviour.

Several months passed until one weekend Maria gave a loud whoop from within the depths of the house and ran out on to the balcony waving a colour coded piece of litmus paper, which she assured them indicated that she was pregnant. Everyone gathered around to congratulate her, Frank somewhat restrained and less effusive, each one of them positive in his own mind that the prospective baby was his. She had missed two periods, an indication that, within the bounds of possibility, all were liable.

The weeks flew by with each one vying with the others in providing layettes, cot, pram and all the other necessities of the occasion. They were all solicitous and pampered Maria who seemed to blossom and glow with health, and in their eyes she appeared to become more beautiful as the pregnancy progressed.

It was a weekend in September, when Maria was seven and a half months into her pregnancy, when she suffered stomach pains and retired to her bed in the cottage. During the night she began to lose a small amount of blood and four prospective fathers went into panic mode. By daylight the seats had been dropped in the wagon and a mattress fitted into the back. At their insistence Maria was carefully carried out and made comfortable on the mattress. They started off for the hospital at a slow pace. Whilst Marie waited a deputation hurried inside to get assistance. A doctor arrived together with two orderlies complete with a gurney and Maria was gently laid on it and wheeled into the gynaecology wing, together with her guard of honour. The four men were directed to the waiting room and Maria was wheeled into a private area for an examination.

For two hours all four men paced up and down; sat with head bowed or whispered quietly, each showing all the signs of a concerned parent. Eventually a gowned figure approached asking for the father. Each one of them began to rise before three of them sank back, allowing Jesse to follow the doctor. They were all immersed in their own private misery, convinced that the possible tragedy was his alone. Half an hour later Jesse reappeared, looking quite distraught, to inform them that Maria had lost the baby. They were all stricken and close to tears. Frank cursed himself for his additional sense of relief as they filed in to the room where Maria was propped up on pillows, pale and quietly sobbing. Jesse sat on a chair by her side and the rest stood around, all desperate to hold her and comfort her. Each had a feeling of a terrible loss, made all the worse by the fact that they were unable to share it and give ownership.

Maria looked at each one of them, noting their distress, their faces distorted through her tears and her heart went out to them. "I'm so sorry," she whispered. "I should have taken more care."

After a while Jesse, who had been lightly brushing the hair from her face, took her hands in his, and smiling gently, murmured "Never mind Maria, the doctor says there's no permanent damage done, you can still have children. Hurry up and get better and we can all start making another."

A Near Gaffe

It was a chilly day in July when Tom and Jenny moved into their new home. It was quite a small place situated on the shores of Lake Macquarie. Tom had only retired a few weeks previously but Jenny, being a few years younger, had some time to go before being eligible for a pension – anyhow, she still enjoyed her work as a secretary at the university and was not yet ready to retire.

Tom was well prepared for retirement, there were a number of things that interested him that a lack of time had prevented him from indulging. With his new-found freedom he had every intention of pursuing those interests. Some years earlier he had discovered an artistic bent that had failed to blossom because of a lack of continuity of effort. Then, of course there was his passion for golf and an embryonic interest in gardening; the nearest he had got to that was to listen to 'Gardening Australia' on the ABC every Sunday. Having spent most of their married life in apartments, their horticulture consisted of a flower-box on the kitchen window-sill.

Tom had been an engineer, so setting out the proposed garden was not too difficult. After several changes and numerous consultations with Jenny the final plan was agreed upon and Tom got to work.

He soon discovered that the new demands on his older muscles were somewhat taxing, so he divided his time between gardening and painting. Sometimes, if things were going well he would forget the garden completely for several days as he strove to capture on canvas some image gleaned from his memory.

Every day or so he would write out a shopping list and walk to the shopping centre about half a mile away. He could have taken the car but he felt that he needed the exercise. The walking track along the edge of the lake afforded a pleasant view of a multitude of motor-boats and yachts; kids fishing off the jetty, and the more energetic cycling or jogging. After a few weeks it became almost a necessity that cleared his head and loosened his joints.

One day whilst on his walk, he noticed a neighbour whom he recognised as living across the road in their cul-de sac. He was sitting on a bench reading a newspaper. Tom called out a cheery 'good afternoon' and continued on his way. He met him again several days later in the supermarket and passed the time of day for a few moments. After the third such encounter he introduced himself and discovered that the man's name was Bob and that he was married to a woman called Joyce. He conveyed that information to Jenny after dinner that night. She looked at him askance for a while, waiting. Tom looked at her puzzled, noting that she appeared to have a problem. He asked her if anything was wrong. She gave a snort and raised her eyebrows. "Well!" She demanded. "What does he do? Does he have a job? What does his wife do? Does she work?" All questions that Tom could not answer.

"We only talked for a few moments! It wasn't exactly a national quiz show."

"Typical male!" She complained. "They never bother to find out all the interesting things."

The next time Tom bumped into Bob was outside his own house, so he invited him in for a beer. He tried to direct the conversation around to Bob's situation but as he appeared somewhat reticent Tom switched to the local rugby team's performance, always a good topic in the area. He realised that Jenny would scoff at what she conceived as a male failing so he refrained from mentioning the latest encounter. Three days later Bob intercepted Tom in the street and reciprocated with an invite into his home to enjoy a 'home brew'. Tom thought that at least he could satisfy Jenny's curiosity as to the furniture – something he would not normally notice.

Bob showed him around the garden, pointing out all those

important and very clever things that look so mundane to anyone else, then they sat in the lounge and Bob fetched a couple of beers. They seemed to have a number of things in common and the conversation flowed easily as they warmed to each other's company.

They were into their second glass when Tom caught sight of something crawling across the floor at the periphery of his vision. He was slightly startled and a little nauseated to see a cat, shaved to bare skin from the waist back, dragging itself laboriously across the carpet. Bob saw the expression on Tom's face and began to explain. He seemed uncomfortable and his comments were clipped and somewhat defensive.

He explained that the cat had become paralysed not long after birth and as it was incapable of cleaning itself properly they kept the hair shaved for hygienic reasons. From the waist up it appeared as a rather handsome Persian but its wasted lower half dispelled any claims to beauty. Tom felt the rising emotion of distaste and wondered why they hadn't taken the easy way out and had it put down. It would probably be doing the animal a favour, he thought. He was about to suggest just that, but as he glanced at Bob he saw a look of sadness pass fleetingly across his face and he refrained. He realised that at that moment Bob was feeling surprisingly emotional. Tom felt somewhat embarrassed. After all it was only a cat! He tossed back the last of his drink and, muttering something about 'getting back to the garden', made his exit.

It was a couple of weeks later when he next saw Bob. He was sitting on the same bench reading his paper. Tom felt an incipient rush of *deja vu* as he called "Good afternoon! Nice weather we're having." Bob smiled as he folded his paper and rose to join Tom in his walk to the shops. The subject of Bob's wife had never arisen previously – much to Jenny's chagrin, Tom having been primed to raise the subject.

"Your wife still working is she, Bob?"

"No!" Bob replied. "She's over at her mother's at the moment; I'm expecting her home next week"

"Oh!" Said Tom. "You'll be glad to have her back no doubt; not easy on your own is it." He smiled. Like most men he was hesitant about asking personal questions. He had already gone further then he liked, on Jenny's behalf, so he changed the subject, knowing as he did so what her reaction would be.

On their return Bob again insisted on Tom joining him on his porch for a beer. He stowed his groceries and ambled over to find Bob already ensconced in a wicker chair with the beer on the table. Tom was halfway through his drink when he saw, with the same distaste, the cat drag its way to a dirt box in one corner of the room. Bob was all apologetic as he unhooked a cloth hanging from a nail and dipping it into a bucket of water, obviously kept there for that purpose, wiped the lower half of the animal's back. He disappeared into the house to wash his hands, Tom assumed, and a few minutes later rejoined him.

"Quite a lot of work looking after that cat!" Tom said. He was about to suggest that it would probably be better for both Bob and the cat if he had it painlessly put down. But he choked back the comment. After all, it wasn't his problem.

It was a couple of days later. Tom had seen Bob leave his house some time previously and assumed he would be sitting on his usual seat reading his paper. It was a fine, warm day and he decided that a spot of gardening would be in order. He was collecting his tools and loading them into the wheelbarrow when he heard the ferocious barking of a dog from across the road. On investigation he discovered that Bob's cat was fighting a very one-sided battle against a small terrier from down the road. As he watched he saw the greatly handicapped cat drop off the edge of the porch and fall to the ground where it struggled with great courage to defend itself. Tom grabbed a spade and went to its assistance, driving the dog off with a couple of well-placed slaps.

The cat lay on the ground in a most distressed state and it was a few minutes before it would let Tom touch it. Talking to it quietly, he managed to pick it up by the scruff of the neck and gently deposit it on the porch in the shade. It wriggled itself into a comfortable position and began washing those places that it could still reach.

'It's just not fair on the animal,' he thought. 'It really should be put out of its misery'.

The next day Bob saw Tom working in his garden and wandered over to see how he was getting on. After a tour around explaining what he was planning to do he invited Bob in for a cup of tea. Bob thanked him, but refused explaining that his wife would be home in a few minutes. Tom smiled and made a comment to the effect that at last the big day had arrived.

"That's great, Bob. I look forward to meeting her and it'll give Jenny somebody to talk to. I'll see you later."

Tom had just finished his lunch when he heard a car draw up across the close. He walked over to the window and saw Bob go into the garage; his wife was still sitting in the car. He watched as Bob set a small ramp against the doorstep, and walking back into the garage appeared with a wheelchair. Tom watched with an awful comprehension as Bob helped his wife gently into the seat. Then, kneeling on the hard road in front of her wheelchair, he hugged her to him and gave her a loving kiss. They laughed as he pushed her up the ramp and into the house.

The Jolly Belle

The war in our particular part of Africa was not going too well. We were being attacked from the north, the west and the east. The only border we didn't have to defend was to the south where the Limpopo River separated us from South Africa. For years, before the war had closed the border to us, the golden beaches around Beira on the east coast of Mozambique had been the Mecca for thousands of sun and sand worshipers from our land-locked country; those who owned yachts and motor-launches berthed them there ready for use several times a year. With the advent of the war and the ensuing sanctions these vessels had been impounded by the local authorities, eventually to be sold off or confiscated by government officials.

Approached one day by my scuba diving pal, Ray, on behalf of the owner of one of these boats, I was told of a proposition aimed at recovering his vessel; I immediately joined them.

Robert, the owner, had been an Air Rhodesia pilot; he had lost one eye whilst playing golf. The subsequent insurance, compensation and long service payouts had enabled him to start up a construction business, about which he had known little; but he had gathered together experts in the field who soon turned the company into a thriving business. He was fortunate in that his wife had inherited a small fortune from her father and this was invested in the company which accelerated its success. Robert, being a pilot himself encouraged his wife in that pursuit and to that end had encouraged his best friend to teach her – his flying days having been terminated as a consequence of losing the sight of one eye - this, he thought, would give them a common interest.

His boat was an ex Royal Navy Dark Class Motor Torpedo Boat; originally manufactured by Vospers of Portsmouth. After World War Two they had removed the powerful Napier Deltic, 16 cylinder engines and sold the boats off cheaply. Most had been snapped up and fitted with smaller engines and converted into cruise boats. Robert had an extra fly bridge fitted as part of the conversion. His vessel was named "Jolly Belle".

One of Robert's pilot friends had a small Cessna aircraft and it was arranged that he would fly us as close to the Mozambique border as possible, together with our gear. He managed to get us to within five miles of the border and only about fifteen miles from the Portuguese town of Villa de Manica. We crossed the border just before midday and made our way to the town which we reached in the late afternoon. We had no particular concerns as there were many Europeans in the country at that time and we blended in quite well. After a meal we sought out a small hotel and booked in for the night and early the next morning we caught a bus which delivered us to Beira on the east coast.

Up to this point we had more than our fair share of good fortune; that was to change. Whilst standing on the beach of a small sheltered bay, gazing out to where the boat lay at anchor we were approached by several soldiers who asked what we were doing and to show some identity. We explained that we were only out for the day and had forgotten our papers. Ray dug into his pack and produced several packs of cigarettes and began handing them around and their attitude changed immediately. After a couple of loaves of bread and a tin of steak had changed hands they became quite friendly and they walked off leaving us to our own devices.

Robert cupped his hands and called out several times until the native caretaker, Ticky, appeared on deck. We indicated that we wanted to get on board and watched as he lowered the dinghy from the davits and rowed ashore. He was effusive in his greeting and we had the impression that he had kept very much to himself over the previous year so as not to draw attention to himself or the boat. On board we soon discovered that there was not sufficient fuel for the contemplated trip to Tulear (now called Tuliara) in Madagascar, which we estimated would necessitate a journey of some six hundred miles via the low–lying island of Ile Europa, most of which is a mere 6m above sea level and is one of the last breeding grounds of the green turtle and a sanctuary for many bird species; but difficult to spot in a turbulent sea.

We were lucky in one respect in that there was a garage just a hundred meters around the bay so once again we rowed ashore where Robert negotiated the purchase of a 44 gallon drum of diesel, which we rolled down to the beach and with extreme difficulty managed to get it out to the boat and hoist it on board using the small topping lift. Having decanted it into the fuel tanks we hastily cast off and immediately headed eastward in an attempt to clear Mozambique waters before we were stopped by the navy or customs.

Jolly Belle was a lovely vessel but maintenance had been somewhat haphazard and most of her equipment appeared to be in need of lots of TLC. Robert was of the opinion that we were averaging fourteen knots but a beer bottle tossed ahead of the boat and timed along the length suggested to me that we were doing nearer to ten knots. As this was disputed by Robert I made no further comment.

Tulear lies on the Tropic of Capricorn on the south west side of Madagascar and was our first port of call on our way to Mauritius; we breathed easier when we passed the limit of Mozambique's territorial waters and set a course for Tulear, which lay in the southeast corner. A quick check of the navigational aids proved to be somewhat abortive so we relied mainly on dead reckoning which consisted primarily of an easterly course which would allow for the southerly drift of the Agulhas Current and an offset for wind drift. There was no compass correction card so we could not allow for deviation but the variation was entered on the compass rose of a very old chart, so we could correct for that.

We motored through the night, taking turns at the helm and sighted the low outline of Ile Europa some hours later which put our speed at approximately twelve knots, which was somewhere between our two estimates. The following day we entered Tulear harbour and tied up at the jetty. A short while later we were visited by customs, immigration and health officials and after some heated discussion the boat was impounded and we were placed under arrest. Having no ship's papers or proof of ownership we were accused of piracy. We learned from Ticky that the Mozambique police had confiscated the papers of all the foreign vessels at the outbreak of the war.

We were locked up in the local brig, which consisted of several cells some four metres square with a couple of benches on either side and a bucket in one corner. The cell already had two occupants who lay on the floor snoring stertorously and who reeked of cheap beer. Luckily the roof was raised a few centimeters above the wall which let in some fresh air – also a host of flies that buzzed angrily around the bucket. We were not housed there long and were released to live on board the boat, but still under arrest.

At all times of the day and night we were besieged by girls and women of all ages, many of them extremely beautiful. There was an exotic blending of French, African, Chinese and many other nationalities that made for a strange mixture. Black girls with blonde hair and blue eyes; white women with crinkly black hair and brown eyes, all offering their services, which we declined regretfully, having been assured of the high rate of disease prevalent on the island and having no real desire to use them.

As we had no power on board we were offered the facilities of a French boat, The Catfish, further down the jetty for washing and showering – an exercise that proved quite enlightening. It appeared that the crew of Catfish had none of our scruples and virtually every door that you opened revealed a scantily clad female who unabashedly followed us into the showers; much to Robert's embarrassment.

We were lucky to be placed under the care of an American official who stood surety for us and who showed us some of the island and took us to a bistro and dance. His wife was a Eurasian mix of French and Chinese and was one of the most beautiful women I have ever seen – sensibly, he kept a close eye on her. We had nothing to offer him for his generosity so I promised to send him one of my paintings – a promise that I regretfully failed to honour; as later events will, I hope, excuse.

A week later, having obtained release via the South African embassy in Antananarivo, the capital, we prepared to renew our voyage. I was reluctant to leave as there were many places I would have liked to visit. Madagascar is the forth largest island in the world and is the home of five percent of the world's plant and animal species – more than eighty percent of which are native to the country. It is also the home of the lemur infraorder of primates, six species of baobab trees and many other exclusives; but it was not to be. Whilst we were preparing the boat for departure and loading a spare drum of fuel onto the deck a man approached me, his furtive manner invited my interest. He explained that he owned a large sugar plantation which employed over three hundred labourers and because of this the new revolutionary government would not permit him to leave and rejoin his family in Reunion. He hoped to join us and was prepared to leave everything behind. All he had was what he was wearing; a pair of old corduroys, a khaki shirt and sandals. He also appeared to have a money belt secured under his shirt and around his waist. I introduced him to Robert who asked me to hide him somewhere below deck as the police were arriving soon and would be entertained with drinks on the fly-bridge. I stowed him in the forward head and suggested he keep very quiet.

We set off early the following morning and headed southward to round the island at Cap Sainte Marie after which we would set a course for Reunion in the Mascarene Islands, a distance of approximately seven hundred and fifty miles; a long way to find a small island by dead reckoning. Apart from the compass our navigational equipment was nonexistent, except for a few very old charts and a DF radio that had been serviced prior to leaving – we later discovered that it was set 90 degrees out, an error that would cost us dearly. We rounded Cap Sainte Maria and left Faradofay about ten miles off on our port beam and set a course NE for Reunion.

We were now in the Indian Ocean with about 7000miles of fetch stretching all the way to Australia; a distance that allowed winds and waves to build up unrestrained by land masses. We were on our second day when the sea patterns began to change and the skies to darken. The signs were ominous and we went around securing all loose gear and battening down anything that could shift – yet we were unprepared for the hurricane that came whistling out of the south, pushing ahead of it mountainous seas that crashed over the boat and spurted in through every minute opening. Soon everything was drenched and we clung to any stanchion capable of supporting us as Jolly Belle aired her keel and disappeared under each succeeding wave, where she seemed to poise as if to make up her mind whether to continue the plunge or rise to the occasion. Eight hours later we passed through the eye of the storm and battled to pump out the water that was up to the cabin sole, its weight increasing the roll and hindering the recovery as the boat struggled to an even keel.

Both motorised bilge pumps failed and we resorted to hand bailing; a strenuous job as the buckets had to be handed up to those on deck to empty. We managed to bail out about two tons of water before the eye passed and the ordeal recommenced. We had no time for food and the effort of bailing and trying to keep on our feet taxed us to the limit and it was with a great sigh of relief that some six hours later the storm passed. We slept where we could on wet bunks and in wet clothes and managed to get some hot food and drink before the hurricane – having completed a figure of eight - hit us again. This time it seemed determined to wreck us. We learned later that seven boats, some of them cargo vessels, had foundered in the same storm. This time it was of shorter duration but more vicious and the entire fly-bridge began to loosen and flex alarmingly; had that broken free there would have been no hope as the seas would have filled us in minutes.

However the storm eventually left us and headed on its way north although the seas were still huge and the winds gale force for two more days.

Between the spindrift and the rain lashed clouds visibility was down to half a mile but in a brief gap ahead I saw the indistinct outline of mountains that I was sure was Reunion. I told the others but in spite of everyone searching for some time we never saw it again. Robert was convinced that I must have been mistaken and confused a cloud formation with mountains as his DF suggested that the island was in fact on our port beam. We followed that bearing for some hours and then Robert picked up a signal from Mauritius which again set us heading northwards. Because of the incorrect setting we continued heading on a tangent to our required course as we rounded the unseen northern tip of Mauritius and headed down into the Southern Indian Ocean – until we finally ran out of fuel.

Extract from log.

'The closing down of the starboard engine sounded like the first nail being driven into our coffin, however everyone is cheerful and with the easing of the weather we started thinking of survival. Using a white polythene bag we stitched on some red bunting using fishing line and made a fairly useful 'F' flag; which is the international "I need assistance" flag and hoisted it on the jack stay. Ray suggested we do the same on the cabin roof in case an aircraft flew over. We got some red anti-fouling and painted a red diagonal on the white roof, not an easy job when swinging in an arc of sixty degrees. Next we tackled the hatch covers which had been broken during the last five days of storms; however the wood was rotten and we made a poor show. We hope to cover them with canvas later. A heavy swell persists which makes cooking and eating difficult but the strong force four is blowing us westward, where we hope to eventually reach the African coast."

Two days later.

"We arranged watches throughout the night but saw nothing. The wind increased and we were thrown around a lot; it was also very cold. Port engine idling but bilge pumps not working – water seems to be pouring in from somewhere. Took several hours to lower level. Both hand pumps have punctured diaphragms. Spent morning patching and have got one in action – however water level still rising. Bailing all day. Managed to remove motorised bilge pump with great difficulty and replaced worn impellor. Bilge pump working and managed to lower water level in all compartments. Seas rough and a strong wind is blowing us westward. Fuel almost gone. Closed down port engine at

1130 GMT. Everyone feels the loss and the silence is deafening. Each one seems absorbed with his own thoughts – and we drift. I asked Maurice, our passenger if he wished he was back in Madagascar but he laughed and said he was well out of that country and looking forward to seeing his family."

Next day.

'Discovered broken pipe in forward toilet which was the main cause of us taking in water. Robert sealed it with a wooden bung and we bailed – and bailed – all day. Not a ship in sight. Ray and I dropped over the side in wet suits and diving gear to inspect the hull for leaks, found nothing. Ray saw a fish but failed to spear it. Discovered two daylight flares and one night flare – both with an expiry date that indicated that they were eight years out of date; stowed them on bridge together with a mirror for possible helio signals. Ray cannibalised all the torches and came up with one serviceable. We also made up a signal flare on the end of a spar using cotton waste dipped in diesel. Robert has suggested we lash a gas cylinder on the stern deck and we have set the regulator at its highest – I hope it doesn't blow up when I light it.

Bad news (yes, more) we have used up most of our vegetables in a stew before they become inedible and our forward water tank has been fouled by salt water. This constituted our main supply and we now have only 5 gallons in a drum.'

Four days later.

'Saw a fish alongside the boat, both Ray and I jumped over with our spear guns but were unable to spear it. Had difficulty returning to boat due to the rapid drift. Replaced searchlight on roof – this having come adrift in the storm. Repaired bilge pump (again) and pumped out bilge. Weather worsening and barometer dropping, prepared boat for possible storm. Ray managed to pick up RGC Salisbury and we listened to music until closedown; all very nostalgic. Turned in at 0200hrs; bedding and clothes still wet. Had a short downpour and managed to catch about five liters by rigging up a canvas sheet feeding into a bucket, unfortunately it was brackish due to the salt on the canvas but we used it in small quantities. It was somewhat upsetting to hear the radio from Salisbury – the wind howling and we all huddled around the radio as if we were listening to a major policy speech. We have grave doubts as to whether a search has been initiated and even if it had we are over three hundred miles off any known course and the search would be many miles to the west. Not one ship has been sighted, nor will there be until we drift into a sailing lane, very depressing. We are now limited to a small bowl of mealie porridge with condensed milk twice a day. As we have plenty of gas I have been experimenting with salt water in a pressure cooker with a small hose from the relief valve to a cup of water; also have a pot of salt water boiling away with a metal plate rigged above it and tilted to catch the condensation in a cup. It is tedious but quite successful. Still no ships. As an exercise in enforced patience this must be unique.' My log ends here.

I was lying in my bunk just after midnight when Ray yelled that he could see lights on the horizon. We all dashed up on deck where Ray was flashing the torch in the hope of attracting attention, but there was no change in the vessels course. My experience was that few merchant ships kept any effective watch at night so I had no great hope. However I hurried to the stern and lit the torch using the meths from the cabin lamps to get it started. I swung it in a wide arc for a few minutes until it finally petered out. There was no indication that anyone on the ship had seen it. A small light at a range of about five miles is very difficult to see even if you are looking for it. I grabbed the gas cylinder key and cracked open the valve as Robert struck a match. Luckily we were standing well back as a flame shot up into the air about eight feet. We let it run for about two minutes but as the top of the cylinder was getting very hot we eventually closed the valve. Ray was calling to ask what else could we do. I called back telling him to get the night flare. It was years out of date but it was all we had. He handed me the flare, it was the old type that had long been replaced. It had a cap complete with striker which you had to remove and scrape the magnesium base, which I did several times without success. Then it suddenly burst into a huge light as the magnesium flared. All I could do was to hold it as far away from me as possible with my eyes tightly closed until it had burnt out. We stood together on the stern deck totally blinded for what seemed ages before our vision returned. Then Ray started leaping up and down yelling "It's turning! It's turning!" We all cheered as the ship came closer.

The ship turned out to be the British molasses tanker, Anco Sovereign and the skipper manoeuvred his ship alongside with great skill, a skill unfortunately not matched by his crew. We set our large inflatable fenders over the side, all three of which exploded as the two boats met. A seaman was attempting to toss over a three inch diameter hemp line which constantly fell short. I called up to ask him to throw a lead line first so that I could draw the heavier line in. This he did but unfortunately forgot to tie it to the other line and it slipped back into the sea. The ship came around again and the crew hung Hong Kong fenders – bamboo sticks tied into a bundle – to act as buffers. This time they got it right and we were pulled closer. Robert explained our position and the crew rigged up a line and pumped light diesel into our tank. All the while the two boats were rising and falling on an eight foot swell and crashing together, the fenders doing considerable damage to the side of our boat. They retrieved their fuel line and Robert attempted to start the engines, however the batteries were flat. The skipper of the merchantman was most reluctant to lower his twelve volt battery down to us in the prevailing conditions as they powered his navigation equipment. However Ray and I lay flat on the cabin roof as it was lowered and with extreme difficulty managed to manhandle it into position in order to transfer the leads. This also failed and after several attempts the battery was returned. The Anco Sovereign had been with us several hours and the skipper was anxious to be on his way so we were cast adrift again with the assurance that he had alerted all the official agencies of our plight and that assistance would soon arrive. We thanked him and his men and waved them on their way. They had filled our five gallon container with water but Robert had forgotten to ask them for some food, so once again we were adrift in the ocean without food – but this time, according to the merchant skipper, we had drifted to within thirty miles of Mauritius.

Later that day a tuna boat approached and the skipper informed us that he had heard of our plight on the radio and tossed a huge tuna onto the deck, we waved him goodbye as the fish was hurried to the galley. Later on the same day a light plane flew overhead and a message was dropped onto the deck narrowly missing Robert, it was tied to a spanner and read:

"Welcome to Mauritius! Have been in touch with Mary and Pat Collins (Ray's mother and Robert's wife) the last news we had of you was leaving Tulear on 28th June. I have booked a call for 11am to Salisbury, to advise all that you have been sighted. Piss-up tonight. Frank."

Frank was an ex airline pilot and a friend of Roberts. This was followed by a further letter later in the day which read as follows:

"Dear Robert, Tom and Ray, my dad is dictating this to me as we are flying along looking for you. The Mauritius gunboat is on its way to tow you home. We have all been very worried about you and hope that the journey was not too bad. We declared you officially overdue over a week ago. We phoned Port Dauphin some time ago and were informed that you had been in Tulear but that you had left. I rang Jane and the Collins' and spoke to Jane by phone and she seemed very relieved. Will pick you up in Port Louis today, cheers, Frank."

The plane flew low over the boat and dropped a food parcel which landed about fifty yards away. I dived over the side and retrieved it. Unfortunately the water had got in and the bread was soggy and the eggs (of all things) were smashed. We continued drifting. We attempted to rig up a canvas sail to increase our drift towards the island but it kept collapsing and we continued to drift all through the following night. Early the next day the plane flew over yet again and dropped a message on a handkerchief parachute which was blown by the wind and landed in the water a hundred yards away; once again I collected it. It read as follows:

"Dear sailors, these Mauritians could not organise a piss-up in a brewery. The gunboat, 'Amar', left Port Louis yesterday at 10am, it lost two of its three engines and got back to PL at 10am today. They are sending the 'Investigator' to fetch you. It left PL at 1300 today and will be coming north around the island. I've been on the phone solidly since yesterday, phoning police, harbour, airport, harbour radio. Jean (Frank's wife) spoke to Pat Collins yesterday while I was circling your position, so everyone knows that you have been found. I hope you have enough food and drink, anyway you should be in PL sometime today – I will come and meet you, whatever your ETA. I hope you have an anchor to drop, you are being blown onto a reef. Will see you tonight. Cheers, Frank."

However that was not to be as further messages dropped two days later informed us that the 'Investigator' had missed us in the night. The skipper was drunk and returned to port. Apparently they had gone to our last known position and had not allowed for drift. We missed the reef and sighted the return of the 'Investigator' the following day. As our Sampson post had been damaged by the lines of the Anco Sovereign we rigged a bridle tow and headed north for Grand Harbour. Twice the tow snapped and was repaired and we finally arrived in Grand Harbour in the late afternoon where Jolly Belle was pulled up on the slipway of a dry dock. We were met by Frank's family and the celebrations went on long into the night.

Unfortunately the valiant Jolly Belle slipped her chocks during the night and plummeted into the dry dock and broke her back. She was a write-off.

Robert organised a flight to Reunion for Maurice so that he could rejoin his family and we all saw him depart with lots of handshaking and promises to keep in touch – but of course we never did. For over a week we were feted and attended many parties before being flown back to Salisbury where more bad news awaited Robert.

It appeared that when he went missing the word had got about his company was in dire straits and that Robert had taken the cash and ran; this was patently not so. His wife fearing the worse withdrew her money – thus ensuring the collapse of the company - and ran off with Robert's friend who had been teaching her to fly. Because Robert had failed to notify the insurance company that he was taking the boat to Mauritius they refused to compensate him for the loss of the boat.

In one fell swoop he had lost his company, his wife and his boat. The last I heard of him was that he was managing a construction company in Natal. I still have one of the silver mugs that he gave both Roy and me. It reads, "With love from Jolly Belle. Moçambique – Mauritius." I will always treasure it.

What am I doing wrong?

I'm bored! bored! bored! It's two-thirty in the afternoon and I'm bored. I know I should not be bored, but I am! I realise that the reason I am bored is because I have not yet learned all the intricacies of running a house and looking after a baby. There are probably dozens of things I should be doing that in my ignorance I know nothing about. My wife will not be too pleased when she arrives home from work, but I hope she will appreciate that I am still learning – after all she has been doing this sort of thing for years.

I am an engineer by profession, tending to specialise in Time and Motion Study and Methods. But last year I contracted a bad dose of tuberculosis, and now here I am after months in hospital, adjusting to the idea that I will not be able to work for some time. Jean is very understanding and we have decided that the best solution to our problem is for her to work as a secretary, her occupation before we were married, and for me to run the house and look after Marilyn, our four-month-old baby.

Of course I realised right from the start that it would not be easy. I used to come home tired and mentally drained after a busy day at the office, but I could not afford to relax and put my feet up whilst waiting for dinner, because poor Jean had had such a terrible day with all the things she had to do. There was washing and ironing, cooking and shopping, beds to make and cleaning and dusting, the list was endless. No wonder she was pleased to take a break when I got home and let me prepare the dinner. I used to think I had it bad until I got home and heard Jean's problems. That's the main reason why I was so worried about our current arrangements.

Knowing this was going to tax my strength and ingenuity I sat down and thought about it for a couple of hours. How would a woman approach the problem? Cutting corners, innovating; planning. I knew I would not get it right first time but I hoped, at least, not to look a complete idiot.

Day one.

I waved goodbye to Jean at seven a.m, making sure she had her sandwiches, money and handkerchief. Then I sat down, head in hands, gazing at my program, looking for flaws and omissions.

Jean had smiled that quiet humouring smile that women adopt when they want to patronise men and I knew instinctively that she was aware that there was a lot missing from my list. I guess she thought it would be better for me to learn by my mistakes because she offered no advice. Well! This is it, I thought. The baby was crying and the house looked pretty untidy, the washing had piled up...I studied my list.

I realised it was no good bringing the baby down yet because she would be wet and hungry and her bottle was not prepared, nor was her pram ready. So, leaving the baby crying, on the assumption that it was good for her lungs, I prepared her bottle and arranged her pram, nappy, bath, powder and towels. I made the mistake of bathing her first then putting on a clean nappy before feeding. I learned quickly; you feed them first, wait five minutes while they fill their pants, clean them, bathe them, dry, powder and fit a clean nappy. Dressed and in her pram she was happy enough for an hour or so. I dashed upstairs, stripped the bed, hung up clothes, collected dirties, vacuumed and dusted, opened the windows to air the rooms and vacuumed down the stairs – top floor complete. The time was now eight fifteen, a little ahead of schedule.

I rinsed the nappy and put it in a bucket to soak then filled up the tub with washing. Whilst that was under way I did the washing-up, tidied the rooms downstairs, vacuumed and dusted. The washing cycle was now complete so I hung the washing out to dry and put on another load. We seemed to have accumulated rather a lot, probably the weather had been inclement, or perhaps the pressure of other work had prevented Jean from doing it. By this time the baby was awake so I spent a few minutes playing with her, checked her pants – O.K. Sat down and wrote a shopping list; time now ten-fifteen, nearly thirty minutes ahead of schedule. Made a cup of tea and read the paper – felt guilty – hung up washing. Checked baby's pants. Wet! Changed nappy. Armed with shopping list and pushing the pram I headed for the supermarket.

Parking the pram just inside the door I collected a trolley and squeezed past four rather buxom ladies deep in earnest conversation. Their deep and earnest conversation was punctuated from time to time by peals of laughter and much backslapping, no doubt they were exchanging recipes and other general information that would enrich their marriage and life in general. I quickly passed down the aisles collecting the items on my list; queued up to pay and packed my purchases into the carrier bag on the pram. Squeezing past the group of ladies by the door, now grown to six, I walked slowly home appreciating the warm sun on my back and thinking of poor Jean stuck in an office all day.

Home again; I arranged groceries in the cupboard. Baby crying; changed nappy. I will have to measure how much liquid I put into her because I am sure more seems to be coming out than going in. I don't want her to dehydrate.

Time eleven-twenty.

Made up feed and placed in cold water to cool. Brought in first line of washing and folded it up ready to be ironed. Filled up tub with last lot of washing, fed baby and put her back in her pram.

Baby crying, checked nappy – filled. I wonder what fearful mechanism operates inside that child to convert that nice looking formula into such a revolting, smelly mess. Hung up last of washing.

Time twelve- fifteen.

Prepared my lunch, corned beef sandwich and a cup of tea. Spent half an hour on the crossword; felt guilty. Got out ironing board and ironed solidly for an hour and fifteen minutes.

Time five past two.

Baby crying, checked pants. Wet! Considered the advantages of a catheter draining into a bottle, rejected the idea and changed her nappy. I realised how hopeless I am at this job and felt quite dejected so decided to take the baby for a walk around the park whilst I tried to think of the things I'd missed. I passed the supermarket and saw the same six ladies coming out. I smiled my 'we're all doing the same thing' smile, but was ignored. They could probably see how inefficient I am. I walked around the park talking to the baby, discussing the concepts of 'Just in Time' production and 'Total Quality Control' – got some strange looks from passers-by and desisted. Back home again.

Time three-fifteen p.m. Jean won't be home until five-thirty.

Decided to clean the windows. Doris next door called out "I wouldn't bother cleaning those, it'll rain tomorrow and you'll have to do it all again." I smiled my thanks but decided to do it anyhow. They obviously have the same problem all the time, their windows are quite dirty. That's the trouble with the pollution; the rain is full of dirt. What a terrible job these women have.

Well, there was just enough time to feed the baby and get her ready for bed then prepare dinner. I knew I had to make it a good one so that Jean wouldn't be too unhappy about all the things I had missed.

Jean came in at five-thirty-five. What a terrible day she'd had. Taking shorthand at meetings; correcting her boss' letters, (he's a shocking speller) and she had to rewrite practically everything. I saw her glancing surreptitiously around the room and ostentatiously straighten a picture that had got out of kilter when I was dusting. She obviously made a big effort not to criticise and I appreciate that. We all have a lot to learn.

Day two.

I decided that as the baby had the same feed all day I'd make up a day's supply and save time. Upstairs did not require vacuuming so phase one was completed by seven-forty-five. Fed the baby and waited for the inevitable. Washed, powdered, and dressed her and put her in her pram. Not enough washing for a load so dusted and tidied, not that it really needed doing. From next door I could hear Rosie yelling at her three-year-old boy. "You do that again and I'll smack you hard. Do you hear?" Then a slight pause. "I've told you once, I won't tell you again!" Then a slight break. "You're on thin ice, boy, I won't tell you again! You'll get such a smack in a minute!" Then, with her voice getting louder with each word. "Just don't MAKE ME HIT YOU! You'll be sorry! DON'T IGNORE ME! Do you hear?" Then; "You wait until your father gets home, he'll take his belt off to you, THEN YOU'LL BE REALLY SORRY!" It all sounded rather desperate, but it's obviously a game they play because it goes on all day. It must be grand to have a mother like that.

It's a nice day so I remove all the curtains, hand wash them and hang them out on the line.

Time eleven-ten a.m.

Doris, from the other side, calls out. "Do you want to join us girls for tea and bickies, Dave?" "No thanks!" I say; "It's very nice of you to offer, but I must do some washing." I extemporise, forgetting in my haste that there was none to do.

"Do what we do, leave it 'till the end of the week and do it all together." I smiled and again declined. I really didn't want to join them. There are five of them who meet regularly as clockwork every day, from Monday to Friday at ten a.m. and at two p.m. It's the best attended group in the street. If one doesn't turn up for some reason the rest spend the whole session talking about her.

Baby crying! Checked pants; Wet again. She looked a bit sore around the nether regions so I wash her and rub some ointment in all the crevices and pin on a clean nappy. Filled nappy! Oh boy! Cleaned, washed and re-applied ointment. Soiled back of vest; changed clothes and put her back in pram and wheeled her out into the garden to a warm, shady spot. Got ladder and cleaned gutters.

Time eleven-twenty.

Cut lawn, trimmed edges and pulled out a few weeds.

Time twelve-thirty.

Warmed up pre-mixed and fed baby. Had lunch and read for a while. Really felt bad. Jean would be furious, but what else was there to do? I had done all the washing, dusting, cleaning, polishing, ironing, washed the windows and curtains. I'd cleaned the gutters and cut the grass - jobs that I would normally do on a weekend. I could feel that I was failing miserably. I made a list of shopping for the morrow and a list of all the meals for the rest of the week. I listed all the debts outstanding, rates, water, telephone, energy, hire purchase on the vacuum cleaner. I made a list of all the books that I should read. I listed all the music I would collect when I was back to work.

Time two-fifteen.

The women next door are having their tea party. They are obviously better organised than I am. I washed the kitchen floor, washed and disinfected the dustbin, changed the baby. Must check with Jean to see if this is normal. In desperation I found the instruction book for the sewing machine and tried out all the various stitches on a piece of spare material. Repaired baby's nightgown.

Time four p.m.

Took baby for a walk and discussed time and motion studies. Home again, fed baby – waited a while, washed her and fitted nappy. Put her into her nightie ready for bed and prepared dinner.

Jean arrived home at five-twenty p.m. What a fearful day she'd had. Everyone in the place is so stupid; she has to run the whole business practically on her own. No wonder she is so tired, but I could see that she was just a little bit pleased and somewhat surprised, she didn't even comment on all the things I'd failed to do.

Day 3.

I'm so bored – I realise this is going to be a challenge; I only hope I can measure up. But then Jean's a great girl and I know she will help me catch up at the weekend – if only I knew what it was I had to catch up on!

The Nightwatchman

Many years ago I was working as a mining engineer at the Tsumeb mine to the north of South West Africa. In many ways the mine was rather unique as it mined both lead and copper a most unusual combination. The Tsumeb mine is only a few miles from the Angolan border to the north and has the Etosha National Park to the west.

The Etosha is one of the world's largest game parks covering an area of 22,270 square kilometres that stretches all the way to the Skeleton Coast. Fort Namontoni is situated in the park about thirty miles from the entrance. The fort has white painted castellated topped walls with a watch tower in the centre. It was built by the Germans during the Ovambo wars and was, I believe, utilised in the film 'Beau Geste'. A few miles away to the east is the old Combat mine, now abandoned, whose other claim to fame is the Hobema meteorite which landed close by, supposedly the largest in the southern hemisphere.

Because of the close proximity of the lead and copper deposits it was quickly recognised by the miners as a treasure trove of mineral specimens. Apart from the obvious collector's specimens applicable to each mineral, such as malachite and galena and many others, there were exotics seldom found elsewhere such as Tsumebite and Stottsonite – named after a one time mine manager. This naturally encouraged many to start collections and the competition became so intense that the miners would take quite unnecessary risks to collect specimens from freshly blasted stopes.

It was here that I acquired my inchoate interest in minerals and gemstones, many of which I turned into jewellery and various artifacts. The collection was later presented to the University of Southampton, where it was on display for some years as 'The David Edwards African Gemstone and Mineral Collection.'

Completing a two year stint on the mine I decided to take some time off and pursue my nascent hobby in the hope of finding a profitable mineral deposit. I packed my four wheel drive and headed into the Namib Desert, heading for the Spitzkoppen Mountain in Damaraland, where after about a week searching I had found agates, rose quartz and a few other specimens before heading off to Gobabis, surely one of the most isolated places in the world. It was there that I met up with a small tribe of Bushmen and stayed with them for a short time – but that is another tale.

My collection was slowly growing and I would often show local natives some samples in the hope that they could lead me to more deposits; often they did. After some weeks I decided to head up into Angola – not a particularly pleasant place, there having been a guerrilla war waging for many years. I drove up to Ondangwa and on over the border to Ondjiva from where I headed for the Cunene River in the hope of finding some river tumbled malachite but had little success so I returned to South West Africa and decided to try my hand in what was then Rhodesia, now Zimbabwe – named after the well known Zimbabwe ruins.

It was a long tiring drive down to South Africa and on to Bloemfontein and Johannesburg to Beitbridge, across the Limpopo River and on to Salisbury, now Harare. Fossicking along the Mazoe River I discovered a large bed of mica schist embedded with dozens of multi-faceted garnets and nearby a deposit of magnetite. I also discovered a large quantity of river tumbled malachite which is quite easily machined and polished.

A week later I crossed the border at Kariba and headed into Zambia where there are many mines, mostly named after similar mines in Australia. This proved to be quite fruitful and I collected the larger part of my collection there, part of which included a beautiful specimen of velvet malachite with a platform of azurite crystals – a most unique piece.

On one occasion I left my wagon and carrying a pack walked along the Kaombe River which runs east of the Great North Road near Kanona in Central Province. It is a beautiful river, mainly shallow with large rocky cliffs on either side. The water was icy and invigorating and I spent many hours splashing my way as I searched for anything unusual. There were many agates, jasper and large pieces of malachite which I collected and stored at various sites along the course, intending to pick them up on my return. I eventually reached a most beautiful spot where the Kundalila Falls break into 70m of thin veils that tumble into a deep pool at its base. I was pleased to strip off and soak in the pool until nearly numb. I dried off in the sun and dressed. Leaving my pack I decided to climb the 100m rocky face of the cliff. It was not my best idea. The first 50m were fairly easy but things became increasingly difficult as I climbed upwards. At one point I was standing on a narrow ledge about eighteen inches wide that passed around a sharp edged rock and curved around to what appeared to be an easy access to the top. I edged along the ledge with my arms pressing against the wall of rock and attempted to swing around the point. I made the near fatal mistake of looking down and saw an unobstructed drop of some 80m. At that time I had one arm pressing the wall to the right and one around the edge to the left, there were no cracks or protrusions to cling to, just the pressure of my arms on the vertical wall. I could feel waves of panic sweeping over me as I froze. After a minute I gained some control and realised that I couldn't stay as I was, I would only prolong the agony so sucking my stomach in as far as it would go I inched around the corner to safer territory to discover that I was soaked with sweat. I made the top and sat admiring the view across the vast Luangwa Valley before making my way back down by an easier track.

I retraced my steps collecting my specimens as I went. Towards the end I had to abandon some of the heavier pieces as they were too much for me to carry. I reached my wagon and dumped everything in the back and gratefully sat down with a fresh brew of tea.

Two days later I had boxed up all my specimens and leaving them with a friendly farmer headed north into Zaire; once known as the Belgian Congo prior to the bloody revolution. I crossed the border at Chililabombwe, where there was a border control complete with a man-operated barrier across the road. I parked my wagon and wandered over to the villa and entered. This proved to be an ordinary house, probably once owned by a Belgian farmer. Behind a desk in what must have been a dining room, sat an official who was studiously picking his nose as he read a comic book; he didn't look up but just extended his hand towards me. I was pleased to see it was not the one used to pick his nose. I handed over my passport which he promptly tossed over his shoulder where it slid amongst several others up against the wall. He looked up briefly telling me to pick it up when I got back. I commended him on his filing system but he made no comment. Returning to my wagon I headed for the barrier where a semi-somnambulant soldier sat smoking a cigarette, his camouflaged cap pulled down over his eyes. I sat there for a while then gave a light toot on the horn. He raised his head and glared at me for a while before lumbering to his feet and ambling over. He peered in the window and asked me if I wanted to change my dollars for francs. I told him that I already had some, He stood there for a while then walked back to his spot beside the barrier where again sat down and lit another cigarette. I waited. After ten minutes in the boiling heat I waved a ten dollar note as he knew I would. He wandered back counting out five hundred francs to the dollar, which was the official rate. Both he and I knew I could get a thousand in Elizabethville. I drove through the raised barrier and onto the strip road. This consisted of two eighteen inch strips on which you drove your car. If a vehicle came the other way you drove off one track leaving it to the other driver – you hoped he would do the same.

Half an hour into the drive to Elizabethville I was suddenly forced to slam on the brakes and skid to a halt as a dozen soldiers rolled large metal drums into the road ahead of me. One, obviously the leader, sauntered up to my window and ordered me to show identity papers. I explained that my passport was at the border control. He stared at me as he walked slowly around my wagon; he took his time. Returning to my widow he asked me if I wanted to change some dollars into francs. I explained that I had already changed some at the border. He lit a cigarette as he slowly walked back to the rest of his men and sat down on one of the drums. I took the hint and waved a twenty dollar note – the lowest denomination that I had. He muttered something to his men and they all laughed. I took the proffered ten thousand francs as the drums were rolled aside and set up ready for the next visitor, I drove on.

I drove into Elizabethville, which was purported to have been one of the most attractive towns in Southern Africa, in the late afternoon. The wide main street had grass growing in patches along its length and potholes sent the suspension rattling. Many of the shops had their windows boarded up and there were burnt out shells on both sides. Bullet holes still pock marked most buildings and every lamp-post had virtually disappeared under piles of garbage that fouled the air with a noxious stench. All in all a most depressing sight.

I walked around the town for an hour as darkness descended then returned to my wagon to brew a cup of tea, then thinking I might find something to eat I parked my wagon alongside a police station in what I hoped was a secure spot and wandered back into town. It was only about ten pm but already everything had closed down so I headed back to my wagon for the usual tin of beans or spaghetti. On the way I passed a green canvas shelter, one of those typical of road workers the world over. Sitting on a rough timber bench was the blackest African I had ever seen; he was so black that when he closed his eyes and mouth he virtually disappeared. I got to talking to him and apparently he was guarding a hole in the road, which the tent partially covered. He had a brazier going and was cooking boereworst – the sausage much loved by Boer farmers in South Africa. They gave off a delicious aroma. He saw my wolfish glances and offered me one, which I gratefully accepted. We chatted for a while and I asked him if he would like a beer to go with his sausage, he was quick to accept. He directed me to a shebeen about fifty yards down the street, which appropriately had a red light over the door. I knocked and was admitted into small room with a candle as its only source of illumination. There seemed to be some confusion as to whether I wanted beer or a woman – I eyed the available wenches and stuck to my original objective. When making the beer the girls sit around in a circle chewing raw corn and when it is nicely masticated they spit it into a large urn where it is covered with an old cloth for several days as it ferments. Then it is filtered through an old piece of rag to remove most of the pieces of corn and then poured into any old plastic containers that might be available. I bought a plastic bucket – hoping that it had been scrubbed after it had been removed from the dump; but I doubt it. On my return I discovered that my friend had unearthed some more, somewhat smelly, sausages and had them sizzling on the grill. We passed the bucket, filtering the beer between our teeth, sucking off the residue and spitting it on the floor.

Just after midnight I was informed that his turn of duty was finished and he suggested that I should return with him to his village. Being in a somewhat jolly state of mind I readily acquiesced and followed him into the bush. The village was only about half a mile from the town and we soon reached it. The kias were of mud and stick construction set in a circle with chief's house in the centre. It turned out that my companion was the chief's eldest son and we entered the smoke filled room to be greeted by many of the elders and the chief who made me welcome. Unfortunately they were also celebrating the New Year and I joined the circle and participated in the bucket passing routine, by now feeling somewhat less than compos mentis. It didn't go on for long and one by one the elders left with much hand shaking and good wishes. By this time my eyes had become accustomed to the dim smoky light and I could see several sleeping mounds containing some of the chief's four wives. The chief indicated a mound near the door, for which I was grateful, and in a rush of unwanted bon homme he offered me the company of his number two wife. I glanced across to where a grossly overweight woman sat grinning delightedly through her missing and rotting teeth and quailed. Now it is considered very rude to refuse an offer of such proportions - I use the word advisedly – so I went through the routine of clapping my hands and thanking him for his generous offer. I thought I saw a flicker of mirth hesitate briefly on his lips. The hag opened her kaross to my horrified gaze. Turning back to the chief I loaded my face with misery and shrugged helplessly as I told the chief that regretfully I had to refuse his offer and pointing down towards my groin I explained that I, unfortunately, had a terrible disease and that I would hate to pass it on. Again his eyes seemed to twinkle as he accepted my excuse and ambled of to his bed. I dropped onto a pile of skins and drifted into oblivion.

I arose early, much flea bitten and hung over and made my way back to the town and the police station car park where I had left my wagon. I should not have been surprised to find it mounted on bricks and all five wheels missing. I walked into the police station to report the theft, which was duly recorded in an old exercise book. The police sergeant shrugged helplessly, informing me that it happened all the time. I enquired if there was anywhere where I could buy replacements. His brow furrowed as his thought processes clicked into action. Finally he remarked that I was lucky because one of his policemen happened to trade in car parts as a sideline and directed me through a door leading to the back yard. I was introduced to the PC who gave a friendly smile and led me to a shed, which curiously enough contained, amongst other things five wheels identical to the ones I required. He commented on how lucky I was and sold them to me for twenty dollars each – he even helped me to fit them, having just the right number of suitable nuts. I thanked him profusely and drove away.

It just goes to show that sometimes, when you are in dire straits, you can be very lucky!

The Last Voyage

The SS Riga lurched painfully out of harbour, her screws half clear of the water churning a dirty turbulent groove that bubbled and frothed in her wake. Her master, a short stocky Liverpudlian, leaned against the bridge rail gazing ahead with unseeing eyes; a tired weather-beaten man, well past retirement age. He was aware that he would have been on the beach years ago if the company had not chosen to overlook his age; partly in respect for him and partly because they could find nobody else to command this leaky, ill-tempered ancient tub.

Captain Coker's mind wandered restlessly over his long and eventful life, recalling the arduous days under sail as a midshipman – rounding the Cape with the decks awash – fighting for his life as the demonic winds strove to tear him from the yards, a breathtaking fifty foot above the heaving deck where he swung like an inverted pendulum; his icy fingers clawing frantically, yet methodically at the lashing writhing canvas. Then ten years later as Mate on one of the first ships to convert to steam.

A smile moved fleetingly across his face like a darting shadow across a field in winter time. His pale blue eyes warmed as he recalled his disgust, distrust and dislike of the stocky shape of his new ship and the interminable arguments that raged endlessly in the fo'c's'le regarding the advantages and disadvantages of steam versus sail. The younger men had accepted the change more readily but the old hands had felt an acute sense of loss at something indescribable but deeply felt – and they had to take a lot of banter from the youngsters because of it.

The captain's mind was jerked abruptly from the past to the present as a lifetime of experiences instinctively apprised him of the fact that something was amiss. An Arab dhow was angling obliquely across the Riga's bow, seemingly oblivious to the danger. The whole crew were on deck, arms waving, voices raised and teeth flashing as they argued hysterically among themselves.

Captain Coker, all sentiment erased, raised his voice in a thunderous bellow that effortlessly bridged the gap between the two vessels causing all heads on the dhow to swing with startled unison towards the approaching danger. The ensuing panic aboard the sailing craft reminded him of the Keystone Cops comedy and momentarily brought a grin to his lips.

Then a string of invective poured from his lips, the like of which was unmatched on the seven seas, it brought cries of delight from his own crew and struck terror in the hearts of those on the receiving end and spurred them to frenzied effort – an effort which some seconds later was rewarded as the stern of the dhow slipped past the bow of the Riga with inches to spare; the black faces glistening with sweat, induced in equal amounts by Captain Coker's stentorian roar and their own frenzied labours.

The cook, his face red from the heat of the galley, poked his head out of the door to request, in a surprisingly refined voice, if somebody would kindly ask the skipper to refrain from swearing as the paint on the galley walls was blistering – in spite of the fact that there had been no paint on the galley walls, or any other wall, for a very long time.

As the ship wallowed her way slowly out of harbour the crew settled down to their usual seagoing routines. Those on duty set about their tasks with the resigned air of men all too familiar with the requirements of their profession. The crew not on watch disappeared below decks, preferring the stuffy heat of the dimly lit mess to the glare of the midday sun coupled with the searing heat of the sirocco wind that blew without pause at that time of the year. The Captain relinquished the bridge to the Mate without a word and stamped off to his cabin.

The keel of the SS Riga had been laid in 1929 in one of the lesser shipyards of the Clyde. All her life she had shown a stubborn waywardness that had been born at her launching. The Champagne had been shattered against her unyielding bow and the owners and other representatives of interested parties stood in silent expectation. The workers, gathered in their hundreds, sucked in their breath ready to explode into the massed mighty roar that blessed those occasions, but the good ship, SS Riga refused to budge. Then in the increasing pregnant silence could be heard the low hiss of slowly expanding air past teeth as the men lining the slipway released the pressure on their lungs. On the launching dais there were embarrassed smiles and the voice of the works manager assuring the guests that everything would be alright in a moment, as soon as the slipway party cleared the obstruction.

Thirty minutes later as the ship had still not moved the launching party and the crowd below began to disperse; so it was that only a handful of dockers and the slipway party were in attendances as finally, with great reluctance, the SS Riga dipped her stern with bulky fastidiousness into the Clyde for the first time. She was, however, destined to wet her plates in the same waters, with the same seeming reluctance on numerous other occasions in her lifetime.

As a freighter, from a capacity point of view, she was admirable; her spacious holds and handling equipment compared favourably with those of larger and more modern ships, however, to compensate for her large freight carrying capacity all other space was limited. The crew's mess-decks were cramped, dingy, and of the most peculiar shape; fitting into odd corners that could not otherwise be utilised. Across the deck-head ran numerous pipes, ducts, cables and wires and a miscellany of odd shaped angles where pieces of machinery jutted out occasioning innumerable bumps and bruises in rough weather. There was of course no such luxury as bunk beds and hammocks provided the only solution to the sleeping requirements of so many in such a cramped space. These were slung across the mess, sometimes three deep, leaving a space of about two feet between the bottom of one and the top of the one below.

During wet weather as each succeeding watch shed their dripping oilskins and equally wet clothes onto the locker, or dropped them in disgust on the mess-deck floor, the ensuing steam turned the mess into sweaty, foul smelling den and caused rivulets of water to drain ceaselessly in jerky spasmodic dashes down the pitted bulkheads forming a reddish wet puddle along the sides of the mess that slopped against the skirting with every roll of the ship.

Christmas was only six weeks ahead and each member of the crew anticipated its approach with feelings coloured by his personal background.

The Mate, married with four children spent his spare time making wooden toys in the small workshop aft and looked forward with genuine affection to seeing his family again. Bobby aged twelve was a fine lad, independent and resourceful, very much like his father. The fact that he had made his debut three months before his parents had married made no difference at all to either him or his father. Mrs Peters, on the other hand, had never quite reconciled herself to this situation and was constantly embarrassing herself and her friends by never making up her mind whether to deduct one year from her marriage date or add one to her son's age; always failing to appreciate that in Hammersmith where they lived this was neither a unique experience nor even a suitable subject for scandal.

The births of Peter aged five, Dianna four and Jane aged three occurred nine months after Mr. Peters returned home from trips to Brazil, Australia and Peru and had left his wife tired and harassed; thankful at last that at the age of forty-three her ovaries were now exhausted and she could look forward to her husband's homecoming without the dread of pregnancy.

The Cook, Roger Latham, known to the crew as 'The Duke', viewed his return to England with a certain amount of trepidation. The product of wealthy parents of the upper middle class and a public school education, he had decided at an early age that his talents were too unique to be harnessed for the benefit of others and had proceeded, with marked success, to employ those talents to deprive his friends of their surplus capital. Needless to say his circle of friends rapidly dwindled and he was forced to cast his net further afield, finding under the guise of an impoverished son of titled parents easy pickings as an escort to wealthy female American tourists. His graceful manners and calculated haughtiness soon had them eating out of his hand and his carefully designed and engineered slips of the tongue secretly convinced them that it was only a matter of weeks before he inherited a title some importance – not that he ever said so in so many words; nothing you could put your finger on - but still….

Eventually one of his more blatant schemes fell apart at the seams and he was fortunate to quit his homeland shores two steps ahead of an enraged parent and one ahead of the police fraud squad.

Captain Coker had signed him on in desperation twenty minutes ahead of sailing time, having that afternoon dismissed the previous cook on representation from the rest of the crew. They did not mind him being a habitual drunkard but his filthy habits had nauseated them beyond endurance; his final act being to spew inaccurately into the galley sink via the simmering pot of stew destined for the crew's supper.

Captain Coker himself thought about his future with a sinking feeling of despair and desperation. He had nothing to look forward to but the slate roofs and dirty wet streets of Liverpool; loneliness and his old age pension. His father had been a hard working but typically poor seaman and he remembered him with regret mixed with a certain amount of affection. His mother he remembered not at all, she having died a few hours after forcing him into the world in a mist of pain and terror. His father had served twelve years in the Royal Navy; never quite managing to rise above the rank of Leading Seaman. But he was a kindly man always neat and tidy and scrupulously clean – at least until he met Molly, who after a courtship of just four weeks became his second wife. She had been the barmaid in Ship Inn in Cannon Place. She had been a large beefy woman with hair that seemed not so much bleached as having withered in the fumes of beer and smoke that pervaded the public bar. Her sensuous leer and loud laugh seemed to young Johnny Coker to match the rest of her perfectly. He could never understand what had attracted his father to her – something to do with opposites, he imagined, or perhaps his father was too lonely after twelve years of trying to make a home for himself and his son. Anyhow, she moved into their little house with lazy insolence, accepting all and giving nothing except her body, in return. She was coarse and dirty and slowly over the following two years he watched his father bringing himself down to her level and Johnny hated her with fierceness that often frightened him. The only two good things she ever did as far as he was concerned were to present him with a baby sister and six months after run off with a Lascar seaman.

His sister Susan he had loved and cared for with almost a religious fervour, dashing home from school to change her nappies, bath her and feed her and settle her into her cot. He lavished on her all the frustrated love of a lonely boy and more than compensated for any lack of affection on the part of his father who quickly drank himself into an early grave some four years later. By this time Johnny was earning just enough money to keep them both fed and clothed, with the assistance of an elderly aunt.

He remembered now with undiminished pain, even after all these years, hurrying home from the shipping office where he worked as a clerk, with a birthday present for Susan tucked under his arm. It was her fifth birthday and his aunt was giving a little birthday party for her. He had suddenly found himself running and had not known why; but a feeling of dread had been upon him. He had burst into the house, sweat pouring from him soaking his shirt, to find it empty. He had hurried through the rooms calling her name; he had seen the table set with a special birthday cake with five candles waiting to be lit and by this time tears were streaming down his face unchecked. As he had dashed for the front door it had opened and the look on his aunt's face had sounded a death knell to him and his heart had died forever.

Susan, it appeared had been dressed in her new party dress and was swirling around in childish delight when the skirt flew into the fire and the whole thing had burst into flame. Her screams had brought his aunty running and she had tried desperately to extinguish the flames, burning her hands and face badly in the process, but Susan had died on the way to the hospital.

The memory of the following weeks was lost in the mist of near insanity. In spite of every effort on the part of his aunt, his friends and his employers he had remained inconsolable and in an effort to help him a few strings were pulled and he found himself training as a midshipman in the Royal Navy where the strenuous life restored him to some semblance of normality. He threw himself wholeheartedly into the work as an opiate to his private thoughts and in consequence passed through the course with honours.

His life had been a chequered one; fighting under sail where he had risen to the rank of lieutenant. After eight years he had resigned his commission to join the East India Company as a second officer and over the years had been in and out of just about every port in the world. He had been master of his own ship for over fifteen years – a lifetime of adventure; but lonely adventure. Not for him a host of friends, women and gaiety; he seemed to have no capacity for loving or being loved. That side of his life had died with the advent of Susan's death. He had nothing now except his memories and for the most part they brought him only heartache.

The ship steamed on slowly across the placid Mediterranean with little to break the soul-destroying monotony except the arguments in the fo'c's'le and an occasional fight that never seemed to solve anything. Shore leave in Malta with a drunken jaunt or two down the 'Gut' and a lecherous evening at the 'Newlife' or a more acrobatic taxi ride around Valetta with a girl in the back for good measure; or the more innocent pastime of swimming at St. Paul's Bay, then off again to Gibraltar where the sequence was repeated; different names, same trade; different beach, same water; then the final leg across the Bay of Biscay and home.

The SS Riga left Gibraltar on December the 5th; the weather was cooler now with occasional rain. Tropical clothes were more or less discarded for overalls and jerseys and the motion of the ship grew more tortuous as they drew slowly out into the Atlantic swells and away from the land-locked Mediterranean.

They were almost through the Bay, that tempestuous and unpredictable expanse of ocean, and all seemed calm and peaceful, when the foreword lookout's voice rang out clearly over the whole length of the ship. "Squall ahead on starboard quarter". None of the crew needed the Mate's roar to urge them on. They were well aware of the ferocity of the sudden squalls that could arise in this area and they hurried on deck with the utmost speed and proceeded to batten down the hatches and make fast all movable gear as the first precursor of the storm struck. The cook began stowing his breakables and spent some minutes wondering what to do with the hot pots and pans on the galley stove – a few seconds later there was no problem as they were all scattered over the floor distributing their contents in greasy streams as the ship heaved to the first ferocious lashing as the squall broke over her.

Captain Coker had hurried to the bridge from his cabin at the first call and was scanning the horizon with seasoned eyes. Quite clearly now stretching from port to starboard was a black wall rushing towards his ship at a terrifying speed, building up the water ahead of it into a towering mass of turbulent destruction; the top creamy white and breaking free flew ahead of the rest and struck the ship first as a deluge of rain, sending the deck party scurrying for cover. Then as the ship was completing her turn into the face of the wind the squall struck with devastating fury.

The old tub tried desperately to rise to the occasion, her decks heaved upwards under the force of thousands of tons of water that surged under her keel. She rolled to an alarming angle until it seemed certain that she would roll right over. A cascade of water broke thirty foot over the foredeck and crashed with the force of steam hammer blows onto the cargo hatches. Number one hatch gave way with a crack that could be heard even over the thunder of water and the howling of the wind, and water gushed into the cargo space.

The torrent continued along the entire length of the deck carrying away the starboard lifeboats which smashed into the derrick adding to the destruction. Slowly the ship dragged her way upward shrugging off the mass of water that sought to push her under forever, only to catch the full force of the second wave following close in the wake of the first. Again she went down to the accompaniment of shrieking resistance as the plates grated over each other with agonising friction.

The captain dragged himself with strength born of desperation to the assistance of the helmsman to help him get the ship back into wind, his shouts were whisked away to be lost for ever in the cacophony of howling wind, smashing equipment and surging water. With the ship back on course the captain roared down the voice pipe to the boatswain to get the pumps started in the forward cargo space. The ship had taken on a tremendous amount of water and was taking more every time a wave broke over the deck. Already it was beginning to have an effect on the steering as thousands of gallons of water rolled from side to side.

The pumping crews worked all out to clear the water whilst the deck party endeavoured to rig a tarpaulin over the hatch. It seemed for a while that they would succeed, then another huge wave struck the deck party sending them spinning in all directions and washing the tarpaulin over the side, and the seas rushed in like a miniature Niagara Falls.

The engineers voice, hardly audible, came up the voice pipe, "Can ye noo get rid o' this bluidy water skipper? If it gets much worse it will reach the furnaces." The rich Glasgow accent sounded only slightly flustered, but it was obvious that things were getting bad in the engine room.

Captain Coker realised that the end was near; this was no ordinary squall. That first mighty battering had not only smashed the cargo hatch but had also wrenched the tortured plates so badly that water was pouring in through dozens of small gaps in the hull. Even if the storm abated it was doubtful if his ship would ever make harbour, and he knew that the storm had not yet reached its peak.

Turning to the bridge lookout he gave him a message for the radio operator to check on any ships in the area and to ask for assistance. The messenger returned almost immediately with the reassuring news that a passenger liner was only thirty minutes steaming distance away and was closing with all possible haste. The radio operator had obviously anticipated his captain's order.

With great reluctance the captain gave the order to prepare to abandon ship and sent the bridge party to their stations. As the Mate left the bridge he glanced back at his captain with a look of tender pity; he knew the thoughts that must be crowding his mind - the torture he was enduring and his loneliness and isolation. In his long career the captain had never yet lost a ship and this to him was his greatest pride, his one proud boast. The Mate saw his shoulders droop and a look of utter weariness cloud his face and watched as he passed his hand over his stubbly jaw and shake his head in bewilderment as if he was trying to solve some intricate problem, and then he was lost to view as the Mate descended to the storm-washed deck.

The wind shrieked down the length of the ship and its banshee wail vied for supremacy with the pounding of the waves and the crash of machinery breaking loose below deck. Orders were being shouted and men strove to launch the lifeboats. With the loss of the starboard boats came confusion as the crew sought new places in the remaining boats

As they were launched the crews pulled away from the side of the Riga, straining to get clear before she sank. The boats were only just clear when the water reached the furnaces and a fearful blast tore the side out and she settled deeper in the angry sea. Her bow dipping sharply caused her stern to rise high above the waves, the merchant flag still streaming in defiance from the jack stay.

The men in the boats watched silently with mixed feelings, some with tears in their eyes as she paused a while, then with ever increasing speed slid beneath the waves to her final resting place.

In the confusion of abandoning ship nobody had noticed the absence of Captain Coker who stood in detached isolation on his bridge; tears dimming his eyes as he thought of Susan - and escape from retirement – and Susan.

Hanna

⌒*⌒*

I left the office late that night. The boss, who always worked until the early hours, seemed determined to keep me there as company – I was right on top of my work schedule and had no real need to stay. I finally left him to it at nine-o-clock and started to walk home. I seldom took the car unless it was raining as I lived two short blocks away. It was a pleasant evening and I was in no hurry to get back to my bachelor flat and the solitude. My girlfriend and I had parted amicably several weeks earlier and nothing in the feminine line had appeared to fill the space.

I crossed the road and headed for Jake's Bar which was quite a small place but elegant enough to attract the beautiful people. Entering the low-ceilinged bar I paused to look around, soaking up the atmosphere and at the same time checking out any loose talent. Most seemed paired off except for one rather pretty young woman who was sitting on her own at a table near a corner; I smiled at her as I walked over to the bar to get a drink.

With the glass in my hand I turned to check if the woman had a partner, she caught my eye and smiled a shy smile. I raised my glass to her and indicated that I would like to join her. A strange emotion flitted across her face – fearful yet hopeful, she nodded. I ambled over and dropped into a chair facing her and introduced myself. She informed me that her name was Hanna.

Whilst we were getting to know each other I sized her up. She looked to be about twenty-five years of age, her shiny brown hair was pulled back off her face and piled up at the back with combs. She had a pretty elfin face with large expressive brown eyes and a wide generous mouth. She smiled a lot and after the first shyness had worn off she chatted away with some animation. I warmed to her and began to make my play with the intention of getting her into bed, she could ease the loneliness admirably, I thought.

The evening sped by with me making regular sorties to the bar to refresh the gin and tonics, which I liked to term ground bait. She matched me drink for drink without any apparent consequences – I toyed with the idea of boosting the drinks up a little.

After a couple of hours I excused myself to go to the toilet and when I returned, much relieved, sank back into my chair. She looked up at me from under her long lashes and murmured.

'I was alright until you went, now I have to go.'

A fleeting look of panic clouded her face for a moment, which surprised me, then, awkwardly she leaned forward across the table and with much lurching and effort pulled herself up into a crouching position as she swung a withered leg ahead of her. She didn't look back as she limped to the ladies toilet, her legs going in all directions and her twisted back causing her to bend well forward. I watched in horror and contemplated making a hurried dash for the door but the feeling of disgust at my thoughts kept me glued to my seat.

I saw the toilet door open and pretended to be engrossed with the antics of two guys sitting at the bar, all the while my thoughts were racing as I tried to think of way of ducking out without being too blatant. We sat and chatted for another hour or so, all the while I was hoping that nobody I knew would come over and join us. I could picture the banter the next morning. *Boy, he must be getting desperate, you should have seen what he picked up last night!* Laughs all round.

She seemed to read my thoughts and her hand reached to touch mine as she murmured. 'You don't have to stay with me if you don't want to, I understand.' She was blushing slightly and I could see her lower lip quivering. The offered outlet seemed to make things worse. I smiled reassuringly and told her not to be so silly. I felt bad.

The conversation lagged and I wanted to bridge the gap by tackling the situation head on.

'How did you get your problem?' I asked. Trying to sound sympathetic and interested, she twisted her glass between her cupped hands and her head drooped lower.

'I was fine up to the age of seven,' she said quietly, 'and then I caught polio – and this is the result.' She continued bitterly.

There was silence for a while and I felt a surge of pity wash over me. I sensed the terrible disappointment in her voice and felt a great sadness for her and at the same time I wanted to get away. I was out for a good time and really did not want to get involved with her problems. Sitting behind the table she looked stunning, a beautiful face, lovely eyes and well-formed breast - not too large. I felt an erotic urge to go along with this, but the sight of her grotesque passage to the toilet quickly put a lid on that.

I stretched luxuriously and muttered something about having to get to the office early tomorrow and the walk would clear my head. I explained that I only lived a couple of blocks away. She asked me where I lived and exclaimed delightedly that she lived only half a block away. My heart sank as I pictured her hopes of a budding romance. She informed me that she had her car just a short way down from the front door and suggested that she could give me a lift. I was surprised that she could drive a car with her problems.

She struggled to rise and I pulled the table out a little to help her, she smiled gratefully. I began to panic as I anticipated having to walk alongside her with the eyes of the entire bar watching so I hurriedly told her that I would meet her outside as I had to visit the toilet yet again. She gave me a level look and I knew she was not fooled. I hurried to the toilet as she lurched her way towards the door.

As I left the pub I heard her call out and saw her sitting in her car a short way down the curb. I opened the passenger door and slid in. Without my asking she told me that the car had been modified for her and that all the controls were arranged so that she could manipulate them with her hands. I was impressed.

Not wanting her to see where I lived I suggested that we drive to her place and that I would walk the short distance to my flat – to help me sober up, I quipped. A fleeting shadow crossed her face. She drove into her driveway and parked the car. I thanked her and opened the door and quickly stepped out. I waited for her as she limped around the car and headed for the front door where I waved to her and started to move off. She stopped and turned.

'I don't suppose you would like a coffee or something,' she said, a note of many rejections in her voice.

I saw the twisted body and pictured the embarrassing years of rejection and thought, why not! It wouldn't cost me anything and I felt I owed her something for a pleasant evening.

'I thought you'd never ask.' I called with a laugh. She looked surprised and inordinately pleased. She led me through the house and directed me to the lounge whilst she headed for the kitchen. It was a small house but she had made it look homely and attractive. I could picture the years of loneliness spent in that very room with no hope of a loving companion.

'There's a record player in the corner and a pile of old 33s,' she called out. 'Find something you like and put it on.'

Oh, God no! Not the old seduction scene, I groaned to myself.

'Don't worry,' she called out. 'That's not a part of my seduction scene.' Again, she seemed to read my mind.

She had one of the reproduction gramophones from the early thirties and a large pile of records in a rack alongside. I flicked through the covers and was delighted to find a cover featuring Sammi Smith, one of my old time favourites. I removed it from its cover and without reading the title placed it on the turntable. It scratched for a short time as the needle worked its way into the groove as I walked back to the armchair and settled myself. I could hear the kettle starting to boil.

Take the ribbon from my hair, shake it loose and let it fall.
Lay it soft against your skin, like the shadows on the wall.

'Oh! I like that one. turn the volume up.' From the kitchen.

Come and lay down by my side till the early morning light,
all I'm taking is your time; help me make it through the night—

'Milk and sugar?'

'Milk, no sugar, thanks.'

-I don't care what's right or wrong, I won't try to understand.
Let the Devil take tomorrow for tonight I need a friend.
Yesterday is dead and gone and tomorrow is out of sight

and it's sad to be alone help me make it through the night.
And it's sad to be alone help me make it through the night,
Mnnn mnnn mnnn mnnn mnnn mnnn.
I don't want to be alone, help me make it through the night.

Hanna came into the lounge carrying two mugs of coffee on a tray, the mugs sliding precariously. I jumped up and took the tray from her and placed it on the table. As I handed her a mug I caught a glimpse of tears lining her eyelashes, which she quickly brushed away.

'When I first heard that song it made me cry.' She said with a short laugh, she didn't think I had seen her tears.

We talked for a while as we finished our coffee then I stood up with the intention of leaving. I felt that I had done my duty and given her a moment of pleasure and now it was time to get out of any entanglements. I watched as her face fell and her shoulders sagged with the inevitable resignation. I felt a great sorrow for her and when we reached the door I took her into my arms with some difficulty because of her stoop and held her to me as I gently sought her lips and gave her a gentle kiss. Her lips were full and moist and her breath smelt of fresh coffee. She pulled herself into me and placed both her arms around my neck; I could feel her desire and I was overcome with remorse for giving her hope.

'You can stay the night if you want,' she whispered in my ear.

The record, having started again filled the house with its sadness.

—*Help me make it through the night*—

I helped her wash up the mugs and turned the record player off, then followed her into the bedroom.

She had a large bed and the room oozed femininity. It enclosed you with warmth as if she had tried to make the room her longed-for lover.

'You can have a shower after me,' she whispered shyly.

I sat on the edge of the bed and waited for her to return. She was quite a long time and I assumed she had her difficulties. When she finally arrived she had changed into a pretty nightgown and a dressing gown, I assumed she didn't want me to see her naked – the thought was not appealing. I had my shower and when I returned she had slipped into bed and the bedclothes were pulled up to her chin. Lying like that she was truly beautiful. I slipped in beside her.

She had brushed her hair until it shone and had pinned it up on top of her head. I reach for her and held her close – she wanted to turn out the lamp but I asked her not to, just yet, and I could smell her perfume, it was light enough to allow her natural body smell to reach my nose – it was intoxicating. I reach behind her and pulled out the comb that held her hair and watched it tumble in sensual waves across her shoulders; then I reached across her and put out the light. Her hair lay soft against my chest.

— Take the ribbon from my hair, shake it loose and let it fall. Lay it soft against your skin, like the shadows on the wall—

I tried to get the song out of my mind as I kissed her throat and shoulders, slowly working my way up to her lips that were slightly parted. My foot touched hers and I moved it back. She stiffened slightly and with some difficulty moved her legs back. I cursed my thoughtless reaction.

'You don't have to make love to me if you don't want to, I will understand.' She whispered. 'All I really want is to be held.'

—Come and lay down by my side till the early morning light. All I'm asking is your time, help me make it through the night—

The song with all its connotations whirled around in my head. This poor abused and unhappy child, for that was what she was, was trying to let me off the hook. I placed my finger across her mouth and let my mouth slide down her throat and to her lovely breast and gently teased her nipples. We made slow sensual love and held each other. For this time in eternity she was perfect.

—I don't care what's right or wrong. I won't try to understand. Let the Devil take tomorrow for tonight I need a friend. Yesterday is dead and gone and tomorrow's out of sight —

We lay there for a long time, seldom talking and eventually I watched the early sun slide into the room through the gaps in the curtains. Hanna slept like an angel with a smile on her face; her breathing was deep and even. I eased myself out of bed and dressed in the bathroom. When I returned she still had the smile on her face.

I scribbled a short note, 'I'll ring you tonight.' And propped it up on her bedside table. I kissed her gently and let myself out.

Authors note:
The whole point of this story lies in the last sentence. He sees Hanna for what she is – a beautiful young woman, he ignores her handicap

Christmas Story

Once upon a time in a plush pad in Neverneverland there lived an auntie and two ugly birds called Priscilla and Anastasia. Living with them was an au pair called Cheze. Now it seems that one day the auntie, who looked like the back end of Ella Sphiz, (Ella Sphiz, by the way, was my uncle Joe's ass and he had the ugliest ass I ever did see}, got a letter from some rich geezer inviting them all to a hoolie on his yacht the following Saturday.

The auntie, who wasn't as flush as she could be, dug the idea and passed the word on to P and A. The au pair, Cheze, wasn't even lit up. Now Cheze was of Norwegian extraction and with her blonde eyes and blue hair looked like a Gauguin mistake – but pretty with it. She was kept around the place to keep the fires going and do the general navvying, besides which the gardener liked daisy chains.

When Cheze asked if she could go they shouted at her in unison (that's an Aboriginal dialect), "Freak off ya dumb broad", and "crawl back to your hole, mole." and other such trivia, and Cheze cried like a drain. But, showing her 'bon ton' (which was prettier than most) she quietly set about her plans.

The great day arrived at last after a lot of bustle and activity - and those two dames sure had a lot of bustle – and, dressed up like a Mulawa revue, off they went with auntie in attendance.

Meanwhile, back at the shack, Cheze was frantically paring the calluses off her knees and muttering incantations – which everybody knows is definitely more 'U' than rhubarb. Rubbing two boy-scouts together in a peculiar way a plastic genie appeared saying

"I am the fairy of the lump – what do you want you stupid chump?" Cheze leaped back with fright and fell into the grate (a sort of grated Cheze). Luckily the fire was out.

"Twit!" She said.

"Twit t'you!" Said the genie owlishly. "I am here to obey your every command!"

"Oh goody!" Said Cheze. "Then first of all get those two boy-scouts out of here, they're nauseating."

This being done she then explained her pre-dicky-meant and was promptly bedecked in satins and lace. Being still loaded with soot and ash from the grate this wasn't an immediate success, however it was quickly put to rights.

Cheze was beside herself – a sort of double Stilton – and gazing into the mirror intoned. "Magic mirror on the wall, who is the fairest of us all?" To which the M.M. replied. 'Of all the girls who are so cute, there's none as cute as you, you boot.' Reassured she set forth.

Meanwhile, back at the yacht, all was gaiety and music and the fairy lights cast dancing shadows over the loaded throng. In the dark patches of the boat deck secretive whispers and giggles were punctuated at regular intervals by Anastasia puking over the taffrail.

Just before the witching hour when the ball was at its height (shades of Mad Carew), a hush descended on the throng (Anastasia being empty at this stage) and all gazed in wonder at the gorgeous doll who had appeared.

The rich boy blunder made a gurgling sound, which was not surprising considering the amount of booze he'd quaffed, and stepping forward briskly he grabbed her by the lower band and sloped arms with her. This position changed subtly to an 'Oklahoma Hello' and Cheze knew this was love at first bite.

Priscilla, ecognizing Cheze, (she was a gourmet) dashed up and started screaming like a jackass (?). The B.B. snapped at her. "Can it! Gargoyle!" This crushed her utterly, and that is about the worst place you can crush a woman that size, and she snuck off with her flail between her legs.

The B.B. told Cheze that he loved her and that he fancied her alfresco (which is a piece I know nothing about) and promptly opened a door to one side of the ballroom. Seeing only darkness beyond he pushed Cheze through and quickly followed her. This was rather unfortunate because it happened to be the 'slop chute' and they both plummeted to the murky depths.

"So folks, just remember this Christmas, if you start groping for a Cheze in the dark you may end up in a pickle!"

THE END

Other Books Published by the Tom Edwards

Lethal legacy

Lethal Legacy started off as a novel set in the year 2050; purely fictional. But the situation in which the main character found himself had to be explained in terms of the deterioration of the environment. Weeks of research uncovered an amazing saga of doom and despair; wrong decisions made for the wrong reasons, criminal neglect and appalling apathy on the part of many from the top to the bottom of every strata of society. Most of the incidents depicted in the book are fictional, but many more are fact, frighteningly so. It is a scenario that could quite easily eventuate; indeed many of the events are occurring now and have been for some time. Many of those in a position to help eliminate pollution will not do so because of vested interests. Many turn a blind eye because the truth is too horrible to contemplate, and some feel helpless in the face of such a massive task. There are of course many selfless people throughout every level of society who strive constantly for the betterment of mankind; the weekenders who plant trees and vegetation along river banks, clean the rivers, estuaries and bushland of all manner of detritus; the many environmental groups, some of whom risk their lives to save various endangered species and prevent tree felling. But all too often they lack resources and coordinated direction; this must originate far higher up the corporate and governmental ladder. Inevitably they tackle the results of degeneration and not the causes. There are also many good environmentally aware people in all walks of life, from the bottom to the top, who try to do the right thing, sometimes to their disadvantage. But many of those who really have the power to effect change are apparently not loving enough or caring enough to slough off their indifference to the ultimate fate of their children and grandchildren – because they are the ones who will carry the brunt of our reckless behaviour in the years ahead.

I have kept the central theme as a vehicle to carry the environmental message.

Undercurrent – Sex slaves and vengeance.

This is not a pleasant book. It depicts the worst side of life—the extreme cruelty of gangs that live off demeaning women. I did not like writing it, but I thought it needed to be exposed.

A senior police officer runs afoul of the local boss of an international crime syndicate who has his wife gang banged and beaten up. He vows retribution outside of the parameters of the law and hunts the gang down to exact his revenge. During his pursuit of the gang, he meets up with the brother of his wife, who is attached to M16 who has the same intention. Jason has been ordered to destroy the women-smuggling side of a massive crime syndicate based in America; they team up. The final chapter asks why the police do not clean up this appalling trade in humanity.

The Honourable Catherine

The Honourable Catherine is the sequel to my last book, Jane Sinclair. It was written in behalf of those who asked for it.

Catherine (Poppet) and Christopher are the children of Lady Jane and Sir Charles Cholmondelay, pronounced Chumley. The two have an uncanny rapport that is activated in times of extreme stress, in peacetimes, and during action in the First World War. Chris loses his memory due to a wound incurred during an action against the Germans. Rescued by Poppet, he is lost to her for several years.

Jane Sinclair

Jane Sinclair is the daughter of Angus and Matilda Sinclair, who have a farm bordering on the New Forest in Hampshire. The story depicts life in 1850 England.

Whilst picking blackberries in the New Forest, she meets Charles, the son of Sir Richard Cholmondelay, pronounced Chumley. Sir Richard threatens to ruin her family should she persist with this liaison. She runs away to London hoping to avoid a catastrophe where she ends up in dire straits. She is befriended by an avuncular figure, Bob, who finds her work in a flower shop, the owner of which dies and leaves all to Jane.

It depicts the struggles of a young woman against adversity who ends up owning two garment factories, in spite of opposition to her ideas on the advancement of women.

Reunited with Charles, she moves to Fordingbridge Hall. Charles decides to have one last fling before marrying and sails to Algiers together with the new Head of Mission. The boat is lost, and Charles and the son of the owner are captured by slavers and held for ransom. Jane, hearing of his supposed loss, falls into a coma, where she is force-fed by her maid.

Charles fights his way to freedom, and all ends well.

This is not a romantic book. It has romance in it. It depicts the struggle of a young woman of the time who fights against prejudice and ingrained misogyny. On one occasion, when her factory outlets are closed to her by the opposition, she is assisted by Mrs. Goulden, the mother of Emmeline Pankhurst, and her suffragettes. Her workforce, unbeknown to her, takes a day off without pay to mount a protest outside the shops.

Jane joins them and informs the reporters, This is the sort of loyalty that you can expect when you treat your workers like human beings and not like animals.

When first inspecting her new acquisition, she insisted on seeing the WCs against advice.

Sir, if they are not suitable for me, then they are not suitable for the workers.

There are many twists to this story that cannot be described in three hundred words.

The English attach who turns spy in order to discover where Charles is being heldof the English crew of a freighter who affect his release. The old sea captain who befriends her and of those who would break her. It is a story of many parts.

If I Should Die

This is a story of Africa, shown at its cruelest and most tender moments. It is also a story of violence set against the breathtaking beauty of the land, where cicadas sing their interminable song, and elephants gambol in mud holes.

It is a story of vengeance and endurance, not about black versus white, but of resistance to the winds of change, the drawing in of empires, and the global trend towards righting past wrongs. It is where Sergeant Bob Wilson and his men fight a war they know they cannot win, but fight it anyway, because it is their job.

No Greater Freedom

The setting for No Greater Freedom encompasses South Africa and those East African countries as far up as Kenya. Some of the action takes place in the Comores and the Maldive Islands and parts of Asia.

Police investigations are initiated after the discovery that weapons are being stockpiled in various townships in and around Natal. It is suspected that moves are afoot in the Zulu nation to separate from the Republic and create a separate homeland. The savage killing of a police investigator in the Cape Town dock area throws suspicion on an ancient tramping passenger ship, the SS Galatea. Steve Konig, a detective inspector, joins the ship hoping to find evidence that would prove that the ship was being used to deliver the weapons from somewhere further north. Unknown to Steve, another detective, Francis Mackenzie, a very black African, has initiated his own investigation into a poaching racket operating in the game reserve near the Serengeti Plain to the south of Kenya – the two investigations are destined to merge.